for Dot

with best wishes

Frank Gright

18 Mulberry Road
by
Frank English

2QT Limited (Publishing)

First Edition published 2011
Reprinted 2017 by
2QT Limited (Publishing)
Dalton Lane, Burton In Kendal
Cumbria LA6 1NJ

Artwork by Pauline Henderson
Typeset by Dale Rennard

Printed in Great Britain by
TJ International UK LTD

A CIP catalogue record for this book is available from the British Library
ISBN 978-1-908098-139

To my wife, Denise

Chapter One

The Twitcherlys were a family of sparrows; everyday, common, British sparrows. You could tell they were British because every time anything went wrong, or anyone called unexpectedly to tea, they kept that typically British calmness about them.

"Oh how nice to see you! Do come in," they would chirp, and not "Oh no! Not those wretched Bumblies again!"

You see, they were very nice sparrows and had been very well brought-up. The other way you could tell they were British was that they lived in England, and they understood everything you said to them.

They lived in an enormous, knotty oak tree in the very large garden of number 18 Mulberry Road. Nobody knew why it was called that, because there were no mulberry trees for miles around. Perhaps, as the houses there were very old, there had been mulberry trees there at some time in the past. All the houses were very large and detached, and had enormous gardens of rhododendrons, azaleas, lupins, and forget-me-nots (and many other flowers as well, of course), so this area was a very pleasant one in which to live for all sparrows.

They were a happy family; mother, father, and two fledglings. They were not, strictly speaking, 'tree sparrows', although they lived in one, but were house sparrows. They should really have been living in a nice cosy nest in a house, but they found things

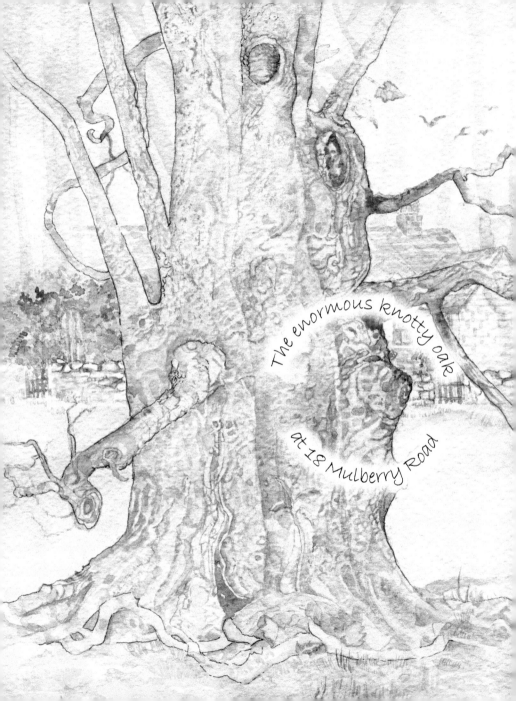

The enormous knotty oak at 18 Mulberry Road

so much bigger, better and more comfortable in the tree. Their home was in a hole in the side of the tree where, some years before, there had been a large branch. This had been blown off during some very strong gales, and the following year the stump had been excavated by a very friendly spotted woodpecker for them.

The woodpecker's name was Lemuel, and he had his home just the other side of the tree. The sparrows liked him, even if he was a little noisy with his hammering at all times of the day. He was very considerate really, because he never disturbed them at night when the fledglings were asleep.

The parent birds had lived in the tree for three years, and up until now had not wanted to raise a family. They had wanted to wait until they had a nest of their own in a nice neighbourhood. Now had come the time, they had thought, to raise their first brood. Mrs Twitcherly had laid her first egg in the early spring, but it did not hatch, and then two or three weeks later, she had laid her other two. The weather had been fine; nice in the sun, but with enough of a chill for you to need to wear a jumper.

The trees were beginning to send out fine points of new green; the sort that looks as if it has been newly painted and is just beginning to dry. The early spring flowers were under way and ready to attract the attention of the worker bees, who were shaking the winter dust out of their wings and making sure they were in working order for their year's work. There were several hives in Mr Bowles' garden, next-door-but-two, and usually there was a lot of activity at this time of year.

There was a great rivalry between Mr Bowles' bees and the wild ones from the open fields behind Mulberry Road. They liked to see who could get to the new flowers first, and which hive or nest could collect the most nectar to make honey. The domestic bees were almost always the best organised and so the best collectors. The field bees were out and about earlier than ever this year to steal a march on the others, and to try their best to buzz the wings off them. They had, unfortunately, woken up a little too early, and, except for a few forget-me-nots and irises, the flowers were not yet out. They had, in the main, to return to their nests empty-pouched.

The Twitcherlys considered themselves very lucky, for not only had they a comfortable and spacious nest, they also had a roof over their heads. This was better than a nest in the usual place in a tree with only branches and leaves to keep out the rain. Sparrows were not supposed to mind the rain, but Mrs Twitcherly was rather sensitive to that sort of thing and easily got rheumatism in her wings if she became too damp. Besides, who could be nest-proud if it became drenched every time there was the slightest shower? She felt sorry for the other sparrows who hadn't a nest like hers.

"Those poor birds!" she would say to her husband. "They must be very wet by now. I think it's about time something was done to provide dry nests for everyone."

"It wouldn't do, my dear, for everyone to be the same," her husband would reply. "Besides there aren't that many oak trees left now"; and there the conversation would end. As long as

4

Mr Bowles' bees and hives

the family had enough to eat, and a roof over their heads, Mr Twitcherly was happy.

The people who owned number 18 Mulberry Road had a little boy. He was a good little chap with a cheerful smile and a kind thought for everyone. His name was David, and he was five. Well, actually, he told everybody he was five, but in fact he was four and three quarters. David liked watching the birds in the garden, and he loved to give them food. He would put out on either lawn or bird table not only lots of bread, but also different types of bird seed which he would buy with his pocket money.

He would sit in the house and watch tits, finches, starlings and his favourite sparrows swoop down to taste his food, and he would chuckle with glee to see their antics. The starlings would push each other out of the way and stand on the bread whilst throwing it this way and that over their shoulders; the tits would hang upside-down from the bird table to eat the nuts; and the sparrows would flit here and there, trying to pick up as many crumbs and bits of nuts as they could.

David, of course, gave them most to eat in the winter when there were not many berries and fruits around, but the summer and autumn in his garden were the best times for the birds, as there were many different types of shrubs giving berries which were delicious for the birds to eat. So, he put out food only when necessary.

He talked to all the birds in his garden, and knew most of them personally and by name. It was he who gave the

Twitcherlys their name, because Mr T seemed to be twitching his tail feathers when he came down to feed. They, in turn, thought he was a very nice boy, and because of that, he would have made a good bird, except that he was a bit too big.

Number 18 also had a cat. This was not an ordinary cat. He was black, except for the tip of his tail which was white, and the tips of his ears which were grey. But what was most unusual was that he liked birds; not to eat, as most of his feline friends and acquaintances did, but to play with and to watch. In fact he got along with most things in the world, except for the holly bush, which prickled his nose. He rarely went near this bush these days, but in his youth he'd had many an encounter with it, and always came off worse.

During most of the fine days, he would sit in a very large tub which had originally been designed for bulbs and other growing flowers, but at some stage it had been knocked over and never refilled with either soil or plants. In it he had a nice bed of soft straw which always remained dry because the tub was in a sheltered spot by the back porch, and was covered by a transparent sun roof. Here he would sit, keeping watch and guard over his friends, making sure no intruders frightened them away. The birds had come to trust him and never gave him a second glance, except to say the occasional chirpy "Good Morning". When it rained, Juniper, for that was his name, would sit in the porch on the window sill amongst the geraniums and tomato plants, keeping watch through the large bay window.

Juniper the cat in the tub. He is all black except for the tip of his tail, which is white, and the tip of his ears, which are grey.

He'd had several fights with intruding toms in his time; cats from downtown neighbourhoods trying to get a quick, free meal, either from birds or from the food they left. He always won, so there hadn't been any intruders for a long time. His fame had spread far and wide, and so his friends could enjoy the garden in peace.

Chapter Two

One day, Mr Twitcherly was away visiting some distant relatives, his cousins, actually, in the woods. They hadn't been as fortunate as him, and only had an old nest in a young rowan. They weren't so well off either, and so they couldn't afford to move to a better area. They were chaffinches and their first children had grown up and found homes of their own. Mrs Finch (for that was their family name), however, had laid another egg, and they were waiting eagerly to see what they would have this time.

"A boy," said Mr Finch, "is what we need to carry on the name of the family."

"No!" said Mrs Finch in reply. "I fancy a girl again. You can dress them up in frilly feathers and make them look pretty."

Mr Twitcherly was a distant cousin, as has already been said, and so he didn't visit very often. It was usually the seventeenth and thirty-second Saturdays of the year when he could make it. This was the first time this year he had been to the woods, as he didn't like to leave his wife too often or for too long. He didn't like to be too far away from his home either, as he felt the woods were a trifle rough and dangerous; he was essentially a home bird, you see. He would defend his home and family very strongly, beak and claw, but it was 'no good going to look for trouble', he was often heard to say.

It was a dismal sort of a day, with the clouds covering the sun, letting only the slightest glimpses through as they skipped across the sky. There had been several light showers already, not the sort to wet you through, but the sort that made you put up your umbrella, only to have to take it down again two minutes later. It was mid-April, and so there was still a nip in the air when the sun was not out.

He spent two hours with his cousins, taking tea with them, and then he made the excuse that he didn't want to leave Mrs Twitcherly alone too long as the children had to be looked after. He left shortly after three and hurried on through the denser parts of the woods with his feathers wrapped tightly about his neck. It didn't do to be seen in this area of the woods for too long where it was dark, overgrown and not very nice. It had been said that there were ravens and hooded crows about, who did not like smaller birds crossing their territories, and so you had to hurry.

On the other side of the black part of the wood he saw several familiar faces in Mr Micah the Jackdaw, Mrs Freebody the Jay, and two very friendly collared doves, Thomas and Jeremiah. He stopped only to say hello as he went by, as they were only acquaintances and not real friends. He did spend a good few minutes with Mr Trog the Wren as he passed by his yew hedge. They talked about the weather, how they both were and how each other's family was progressing. They were generally being polite when Mr Twitcherly noticed the air had suddenly become much colder and the breeze was freshening. The clouds had thickened and already a few large drops of rain were falling.

"Looks as if we are in for some rain," observed Mr Trog. "Hope it's not one of our usual April storms."

"I must be going," replied Mr Twitcherly. "I still have a way to go, and I don't want to be caught in this rain."

So he set off again. He was through the copse and over the winding lane when he was caught off balance by a great gust of wind as he was changing direction. He steadied himself and reset course for home, but the wind had become stronger and the rain was beginning to hiss around him as it swished through the trees and grasses. He began to find it more and more difficult to keep on course, and was constantly blown away from the path he wanted to take.

"I must take shelter until it has passed," he thought, and so he made straight for Farmer Tippet's barn. It wasn't used very much, except by the odd family of owls, but the roof was almost completely intact and there was always a good amount of straw inside its three walls.

He flapped with all his remaining strength against the gale that was now blowing, but he was fighting a losing battle. His wing beats grew fainter as the wind grew stronger, and eventually he was blown along without being able to do anything about it. He hoped he would be blown into the branches of a tree where he could take shelter. He had been buffeted and spun about so much that he now did not know where he was. Finally he came to rest in an old haystack, wheezing and gasping wildly. He didn't even have the strength to lift his head to see where he was. He simply lay there for quite some time, trying to collect his thoughts and his strength.

After a while he began to recover his breath, and so he decided it was time to assess the situation. Very gingerly he popped his head out of the straw and saw - open country with not a tree in sight for miles around!

"Oh dear!" he said. "I don't like the look of this. I don't recognise any of this at all."

He had been blown so far off course, he was now in country completely unknown to him. By this time it was getting on towards early teatime and he knew Mrs Twitcherly would be getting a little worried about his lateness.

"Only one thing to do," he thought; "fly as high as I can to survey the scene and try to find some landmarks I recognise."

He hopped out of the straw and, looking both ways before setting out (for you never know what is about), he launched himself into the air. It should be quite easy, he thought. He had seen the skylarks do it often. But it wasn't quite as easy as it at first seemed. By the time he had reached a sufficient height to see where he was, he was very much out of breath. He could see quite a long way and was, in fact, pointing in roughly the right direction. He could just see the television aerials of the houses before Mulberry Road.

Mr Twitcherly was also being watched; by unwanted company. Just above his hovering body was the shadowy form of a sparrow hawk! There is nothing a sparrow hawk likes better than a nice, juicy, well looked-after and well-fed sparrow (he obviously wanted to have Mr Twitcherly for his supper). The first thing Mr T knew of his unwanted companion was a swish by his ear and a knock on the back which sent him plummeting towards the earth.

As luck would have it, the hawk's talons had not been out and so Mr Twitcherly was only stunned, but not too stunned to take very quick action. As the hawk dived in for the second time and for the kill, talons unsheathed, Mr T swerved and took refuge in a large, dense and prickly hawthorn hedge. He was only just in time! The hawk beat the air with its powerful wings where Mr Twitcherly had been but a second before. He sat on a

Hawk attack on Mr Twitcherly

branch inside the hedge, shivering with fright. He was not made for such aerobatics, nor for such violence. He was quite a mild-mannered little bird really. He thought that the best tactic, when his thoughts had cleared, was to sit still until the hawk became tired of waiting, and then make his escape for home.

Fortunately, the hawk had either another appointment or a more pressing dinner engagement. He circled the hedge for only a short while and then was seen by the still shaking sparrow heading in a westerly direction, away from Mr T's route home.

Mr Twitcherly waited for a little while longer, trying to gather his scattered wits before setting out again. When he thought sufficient time had passed, he popped his head out of the hedge, looked left and right, took his bearings and set off as fast as he could, hugging the side of the hedge. He did this so that he couldn't be seen from either side. He cast wary glances above him as he flew because he didn't want the same experience as he'd just had with the hawk. There were many creatures about these days who would dearly love to have a fat sparrow for lunch or dinner!

He passed the hedge without another stop, and by the time he reached the first signs of civilisation that he knew, he was very much out of breath. As he approached the end of Sycamore Grove, the street about a mile away from his home, he had to stop and take his breath, hawk or no hawk. He wasn't quite as fit as he thought he was, so he landed, a little heavily, on one of the arms of a small telegraph pole. After a few minutes, he was joined by a rather hungry-looking pigeon.

"You look tired and upset," cooed the pigeon. "Can I help?"

"No, thank you, really. I am quite all right now," he replied "I have just had a rather nasty experience with the weather, and a hawk. I nearly ended up on his dinner table. It was only by good fortune that I found a friendly hawthorn hedge nearby."

"That hawk," replied the pigeon with a look of concern on its face, "lives around here and is always attacking passers-by. I lost a good friend the other day to him. Something ought to be done about it."

By this time Mr Twitcherly had recovered sufficiently well to be able to start off again. He said goodbye to the friendly pigeon and thanked him for the chat (he was a very polite sparrow, you see), and set off again. Never before had he been so glad to see the houses of humans. Their roads, lamp posts and cars, which he used to think spoiled things, were a very welcome sight to him. He still flew, with an eye skywards even across Acacia Drive, until Mulberry Road came into view, and with it, Number 18.

The lights were on in the house because darkness had fallen around it. The sodium lights in the streets were just beginning to glow more brightly, and as it was now late into the evening, Mrs Twitcherly was very upset and agitated. She was standing on the small piece of broken branch remaining outside their hole, looking around in a very upset fashion, and she was enormously pleased and relieved when her husband flew in and landed next to her.

"Oh my goodness me, husband! Where have you been?" she burst out. "I have been waiting here not knowing whether you were alive or ..." she paused for breath "... worried sick and the children ..." She burst into tears of relief.

Mr Twitcherly put a comforting wing around her shoulders. "There now my dear," he said soothingly; "no need to worry any more. I'm here. I had such an experience. It all started ..."

They went inside to settle down and have a warm drink. This had been an extremely eventful day for the sparrows.

The lights were on in all the back rooms of Number 18, as the family was having its evening meal, quite unaware of the drama being played outside. The night closed in completely, and Juniper, the cat, sat in his pot watching over all his territory.

Chapter Three

Spring was a very happy time of year for all the creatures, and in particular the sparrows, with their first brood growing daily. They would soon be ready to leave home to find their own way in the world. However, Mrs Twitcherly didn't like to dwell on that for too long, preferring to look after her two boys and be happy to live for the time being. Her husband always told her that one day she would have to accept that they would want to leave to find employment and oak trees of their own, for they had grown to like their home so much that now an ordinary dwelling just wouldn't do at all. It would have to be something very special indeed to measure up to the home they had shared with their parents.

They were soon able to hop about on the lawn beneath the oak tree as if they had never done anything else. Their feathers were almost completely formed, and of course they had as yet to take their first major step - flight. It might have seemed quite an impossible task for the little ones not able to fly, to be able to get off the ground, particularly as there were neither stairs nor lifts in this particular oak, but nothing proved too difficult for too long for these two. They were ever finding new things to discover, and new ways to do their exploring.

They had found (when their father was not available for a piggy-back ride) that it was quite easy to hop from one branch or twig to another one below (oaks are very densely branched), and finally to slide down a curving branch to the floor. The return journey was, however, something more of an ordeal. They hadn't yet learned how to reach the lower branch once on the ground so that they could carry out the reverse procedure in getting back to their nest. So far they had had to scramble about at the base of the tree, making plaintive chirruping noises so one of their parents (usually mother) would come down and take them up one at a time.

Their names were Furtive and Fearless (names given to them by David). Furtive had the habit of rooting about in most things in a very quiet manner. He would much rather go off and find his own food than eat with all the others on the lawn. Fearless was given his name because he would stand his ground (even against starlings) to receive his food. He had even been known to chase away parent sparrows as well as other fledglings in his eagerness for food.

There was such a lot to see and do in this wonderful garden. There were masses of tall plants, bushy shrubs, short-stemmed flowers, and others. Furtive loved scrambling about in and out of the stems of the closely growing Esthereeds, with their long stalks and proud white heads. Climbing the red-hot pokers like the other sparrows to feed out of the opening flower cups and sitting in the thick foliage of the privet hedge were his favourite pastimes. The rambler roses were a little hard on the feet whenever he forgot himself and leapt on to the lower branches. Those thorns really were sharp to tender young claws!

There was a place in this garden, however, which seemed to have been forgotten, or undiscovered by all the others. One day, Furtive was busy minding his own business, rooting around as usual, that he didn't notice he had strayed close to Lady Blackbird. Now, she was a very cantankerous old bird if ever there was one. All the others gave her a very wide berth as she would nip and

The garden at 18 Mulberry Road

peck at anyone who had the cheek to come within a few inches of her private domain. Furtive had been told about her, but he had either forgotten, or not listened in the first place. The first he knew was a sharp pain in his rear end which sent him scurrying backwards, holding on to his tail feathers.

He stopped when he realised he was not pursued, and found that this was a part of the garden he had not seen before. The plants and shrubs were in great need of lifting and splitting as they were so close together.

It was rather dim in amongst the foxgloves, Johnson's Blue and lavender (which made him sneeze violently). The soil was quite moist under foot, and there was the heavy scent of flowering currant in the air making his head swim, making the twittering of the other birds seem far away. He had gone as far as he could when he met an almost impenetrably tangled curtain of flower stems.

He would not have been able to squeeze through it had it not been for a slight kink in one of the stems, big enough to let a small sparrow pass. He managed it with something of a struggle (because he wasn't quite as small as he had thought), and once through, he was glad he had made the effort. Inside the stems was a small bower, large enough for Furtive, with dried grass on the floor and a roof of leaves and flowers overhead. It was the perfect place to come for a rest and to get away from the hustle and bustle of garden community life. This, then, became his secret hideaway, and he didn't even tell Fearless. He would have spoiled everything, drawing attention and generally bustling about.

It was here that Furtive was introduced to worms - as food rather than as companions. Sparrows are not strictly supposed to eat worms, only bread, seeds and berries, but Furtive was pecking about near his hideaway one day when he lifted his head from the floor and found, to his surprise, that he could not open his beak! He made himself cross-eyed trying to see why, and when he did eventually discover the reason and managed to free himself, he found a soft, slimy, thin and wriggling blade of grass there. It did not, in fact, turn out to be grass at all, but a juicy worm. He discovered that, except for a slightly earthy taste, it was quite delicious when swallowed. After that, he became very partial to the odd worm or two to supplement an otherwise boring diet.

On one particular day, Furtive had just managed to get away from his brother (not that he didn't like him, but Fearless did become a little tiresome on occasions with his blustering attitude), and creep away to his hideout, when he glimpsed out of the corner of his eye, a rather fat worm slithering off into a dense clump of lupins. He had never seen one so large before, and so, thinking it might have been something larger than a worm, he poked his head cautiously into the outer tangle of leaves. The smell of dampness was quite strong and the mass of stalk and stem cut out most of the light.

It took quite a few minutes for him to become used to the dimness, and, on looking around, he saw what could only be described as a thick stub end of rope, but which, in fact, turned out to be the rear end of the worm. Without hesitating, Furtive threw caution to the wind and stabbed at this delectable mouthful (it would have, in fact, filled several mouths!). Fortunately for the worm (and perhaps for Furtive too), his aim was not quite as accurate as it might have been, and he scored a glancing blow on the very tip of the worm's bulbous end. This was enough to make the worm sit up, look around and move off very rapidly (all in as much time as it took Furtive to pull his beak out of the soil).

The altercation with Frobel Fleetfoot

It disappeared in a flash of leaf and grass, but with Furtive close behind.

Their chase took them in and out of most of the plants in that area of the garden. You may well ask, and I suppose you have already, how a worm could move fast enough to escape the attentions of a determined sparrow. Well, this was no ordinary worm. He was Frobel the Fleetfoot (which was ridiculous really, because he had no feet!), the fastest living worm, and it was because he was so fast that he had survived for so long, which explained his size.

Furtive may have been a retiring sort of a bird, but he was nothing if not determined. He forgot all the instructions and careful guidance from his parents in his headlong dash around the garden. He quite often came within poking distance, but at the last moment Frobel put on an extra spurt and stayed ahead.

His only means of escape, thought Frobel, was to make for the house. He was very close when Furtive made his last desperate effort to secure his lunch, but, alas for the sparrow, Frobel was just too quick and wily. He shot up the door of the porch and in through the keyhole, just as Furtive pounced. Frobel was again safe to live another day, but the only reward Furtive received was a slightly bruised beak where he had hit the handle of the door.

Furtive waited around the corner of the porch for some time in case the worm should emerge, but Frobel was not quite as silly as that. He was enjoying a much earned rest in amongst the plants on the shelves of the porch, and there he would stay, undetected, for a good while longer.

Eventually, Furtive became fed up with waiting, and he returned to the oak. When he reached the bottom, he simply stretched his feathers without thinking, flapped his wings and flew up into the lower branches. It wasn't until he reached his parents' nest that he realised what he had done.

"I can fly! I can fly!" he twittered so loudly that his mother had to cover her ears with her wings.

"Very good, dear," she replied, "but not so loudly if you don't mind."

He couldn't wait to tell his father and Fearless about his adventure and his achievement.

This meant that both fledglings had learned to fly, as Fearless's attempts had been fruitful the day before. Mrs Twitcherly's calm and off-hand reply to Furtive's excitement was a cover for agitation and sadness. She was happy for her son that he could at last fly, but deep inside she knew that this would mean that they would be leaving home in the near future, as all sparrows who have grown up do.

That evening, when both sons had been tucked up in bed and were asleep, she spoke to her husband about her thoughts and fears.

"Why is it that all sparrows have to leave home soon after they can fly?" she said to him.

"It is the way of the world, my dear," he replied. "They are ready to start lives of their own."

"But they could stay here with us," she put in. "The home is big enough, and you could put on that extension to the nest that you have always promised. Humans don't send their offspring out as soon as they are ready."

"Some of them do, dear," he said in a soothing tone; "but I do agree that some of them do stay in the family home if they wish. You see, you will not have to be hurt or upset if our two boys wish to make a life of their own. Our ways may not be the sort of ways they might wish to follow. They are younger, and they have younger ideas on living. I would give them all the help and advice I could, but after that, it would be up to them."

"You must ask them tomorrow," she said to her husband quite firmly.

"Yes, my dear," Mr Twitcherly replied with a resigned sigh, and with that their conversation ended and they prepared to go to bed.

As they were settling down and drifting into that state between sleeping and waking, they were jolted back to full consciousness by a terrifically loud drumming noise somewhere at the back of their room. It continued for a few minutes, and then stopped.

"What on earth ...?" snapped Mrs Twitcherly.

"It must be Lemuel doing some late evening work," replied Mr T quite drowsily. "He will have forgotten about our strange habit of going to bed at night!"

The drumming continued on and off for ten or fifteen minutes, with their drowsing and waking several times in between. Finally, Mrs Twitcherly got up, and, in rather a cross and irritable tone, said to her husband, "Well, aren't you going to do anything about it? He will wake the boys, and I can't be expected to run a household on no sleep at all!"

"All right, my dear," he replied very patiently, stirring himself from a comfortable and warm doze. "I will go round and have a word with him. He is a little absent-minded, you know."

With that, he shuffled out of the hole, flew up to the next branch and hopped around to Lemuel's front door. He tapped on the tree side with his beak, and, as there was no answer, he hopped in.

Lemuel's hole was not a hole at all, but a series of excavations into the tree. Tunnels led off from chambers and opened out into other chambers. These he would not be using at all, ever, but Lemuel was a compulsive excavator. He loved to hear the sound of his own beak, and would work hours on end when the mood took him.

Once inside, Mr T called out for Lemuel. The drumming stopped, and Mr Twitcherly called out again. Off to his right he could hear the rustle of feathers against wood, and the occasional mutter as Lemuel made his way out of one of his many passages. He emerged just to Mr T's left this time, muttering that he would have to widen that particular stretch of tunnel when he could get around to it, as it was a bit of a squeeze.

"Hello, old chap," Lemuel chattered quickly. "What brings you around here? I don't see you very often, you know. How are the boys these days? Are they flying yet? Do sit down and take some tea. It must be about time for ..."

"Sorry, old friend," butted in the sparrow, "but it's not tea I came for; not for a social chat. You see, you are keeping us awake with your hammering ..."

"Taken to sleeping in the afternoon now?" Lemuel asked genuinely. "Bad for the health, you know, too much sleep. You should try night time."

Lemuel the great spotted woodpecker

"But it is night time!" interrupted Mr T. "It's the middle of the night!"

"Oh dear!" Lemuel said with his wing clasped over his semi-open beak. "Oh dear indeed! I didn't realise it had become so late. I only thought ... Well, there I go again, carrying on without thinking. What you must think of me! Please accept my apology. Must go off to bed now. Can't stand around here chattering the night away. There's work to be done in the morning. So if you'll excuse me, old man. Can you show yourself out?" and with that he disappeared down another hole, leaving Mr Twitcherly open-beaked where he was.

He closed his beak, smiled slightly, and found his way out into the night air. The moon was up, surrounded by a halo of brightly shining dots. The rest of the sky was black and empty. There were no clouds to speak of, and there was a slight chill in the air, so Mr Twitcherly hurried back to his bed, to find that his wife was already fast asleep. He settled himself down quickly before Lemuel forgot himself again and thought it was day. As it was, there would be very little time between his going to bed and the breaking of dawn, when all would be up and about. As he was dropping off, his mind drifted back to the time when he used to be up half the night with the boys; what with settling them down and fetching the odd feed. Ah yes! Those were happy if tiring days.

The next he knew was the weak morning light creeping through the doorway. He was usually the first to rise but he could hear sounds of stirring from his sons nearby. He felt a little tired, but that was understandable in the circumstances.

Both boys appeared as their mother was waking up, and announced very proudly that they would both fly out and find breakfast for them all. When they had both gone, Mrs Twitcherly looked at her husband with tears of pride in her eyes.

"My boys!"she sighed."You won't forget to speak to them, will you?"

"After breakfast, my sweet,"he replied.

The boys were gone ten minutes or so, just enough time for their mother to tidy up the nest and herself. It was a fine crisp morning and the boys had found a great many things to eat for breakfast, and to fill the larder for the day. They had brought back a good deal of fine granary bread (they liked the hard pieces of wheat) that David had put out for them and quite a large amount of seeds and bird food in general. He was a good boy, putting out food every day without fail.

"What a delicious meal that was!" exclaimed Mr T, perching back quite satisfied after breakfast.

"And such a change from having to go down to find it ourselves," added Mrs Twitcherly. She gave one of her looks to her husband, as if to say,"Well, go on then; get on with it", and he, knowing her very well, turned to the boys.

"Well my boys," he started, thinking carefully about what to say, "You can both fly now and are growing up fast. Soon will come the time when young sparrows, such as yourselves, think about starting up on their own. Your mother and I have tried to give you as good a start in life as we could ..."Here he paused and coughed slightly, finding the words difficult to bring out. There was also a little lump in his throat. He cleared his throat and went on, "Your mother and I .. that is, your mother ..."

"But we don't want to leave home, dad," interrupted Furtive. "At least, I don't ..."

"... nor me," added Fearless.

Furtive was their spokesman. "We love our life here; our home, the garden - there could be none better anywhere. We shall stay just as long as you will have us."

Mrs Twitcherly burst into tears of pure joy and happiness, and Mr T stood there with a huge smile on his beak.

"That's settled it then," he said. "We must start that extension to the nest tomorrow. I will get Lemuel to come around - he won't mind - to excavate a little more of the hole at the back, and I - we - will rebuild the nest."

He looked over at the boys who were nodding their heads eagerly. This was undoubtedly going to be an absolutely perfect day, Mr T could see as much.

Chapter Four

How happy the family was on these warm, late spring days! Mrs T had all that she could desire in the world - the best husband (according to her), two fine growing boys, and a comfortable nest. These were the most important things to her, which, along with other less vital items, like a plentiful supply of food, safety, good health and weather, made her happy.

One day Mr Twitcherly came in to their living room with the boys, after a hard morning's work extending the nest. Lemuel had done them proud the day before, having really gone to town on enlarging the rear part of the nest, and the chamber was now three times the size. Mr T had used some of Lemuel's fine wood shavings and a large amount of discarded wool he found at the bottom of the garden to line the floor. This was going to be the best and most luxurious nest ever. There would not only be a sleeping area, but an eating area, and a perching part as well.

"Well, my dear," twittered Mr T, "we have worked hard, and now we need to rest a while."

The boys agreed, and all sat down for a cup of tea. Actually, there was another matter he wanted to discuss, and that needed the whole of the family together. After a lot of pleasant small talk about this and that, Mr Twitcherly cleared his throat and spoke.

"I have been thinking of late,"he started in his official, serious tone,"that it is time ..."here he cast a quick glance at the others to see if they were listening, and they were ..."we had a holiday."

There was a buzz of excitement from the others as they decided where they would like to go.

"The seaside for me," burst in Fearless, although he didn't know what or where the seaside was.

"No,"butted in Furtive,"to the countryside and the woods."

"I think we should all talk about it better than this," Mrs T said finally."After all, it is our holiday, and I think your father is right to bring it up for discussion."

Mr Twitcherly sat down and leaned back with a slight smile of satisfaction on his beak. He had for once made a decision which had turned out to be quite right, and he was clearly pleased with himself. He hadn't, of course, thought that everyone might want to go to a different place. Quiet soon descended on the nest as they all sat back, not knowing really where to start. After a few minutes of silence, Mrs Twitcherly spoke.

"Well," she said, turning to her husband, "the idea can't decide for itself. It was your idea. You tell us where we are going to go!"

"Well ... I ... er ..." he stuttered and stumbled, completely taken aback. He had thought that all he would have to do was to mention the word 'holiday', and it would be decided without much bother. Instead, here he was, stuck without an idea in his head, and all the while his wife was tapping her claw on the floor, becoming more impatient and tutting all the while.

'Oh my Great Uncle Ebeneezer!' he thought. That was a saying he used quite often when he was in a tight corner, not knowing which way to look for an answer.

"That's it!" he blurted out. "We'll go to visit my great uncle Ebeneezer. He lives in the country in a very smart wood with a lake nearby. There are lots of things to do and lots of places to visit, so the boys could do as they wished. The wood is very nice, with lots of small, odd corners for rummaging around. The lake is not too deep, and there is sand and pebble on the shore and Uncle Ebeneezer has a large and stately home in a huge old elm on the edge of the wood. He is extremely wealthy, you know; made his fortune in acorns."

"That sounds marvellous," Mrs T said, "but how are we to let him know?" She was a very well-mannered sparrow, you see, and wouldn't have liked to put anyone out.

"He lives on his own," answered her husband, "and said that we didn't visit him half often enough. He emphasised that we should go down to see him any time."

"That settles it!" chorused the boys. "Let's go now."

"No," said their mother, "we can't go just like that, dropping everything. We must plan, and pack a few things. We will prepare today and set off tomorrow, if the weather is fine enough."

So they all set about their tasks with a will, mainly to while away the time until they were able to begin their journey.

The rest of the day passed very slowly for the boys who were eagerly awaiting their journey south. Great Uncle Ebeneezer actually did not live very far away, so they would be able to fly there quite easily in a morning, but they would have to make several stops along the way for rest and refreshment. The boys had never before been so pleased to go to bed at the end of a day, but once in bed they didn't go to sleep straight away because of the excitement. They talked, quietly of course, about the sorts of things they would do and see, and of course, about the journey itself. In fact, they talked so quietly that they almost didn't notice that they had talked themselves to sleep.

The velvet of night changed very slowly into the sharp grey of early dawn, and as soon as the first light of day streamed into the nest, Mr and Mrs T were up and about. All their packing had been done the night before, and so everything was ready for an early start. The boys were again consigned to scurrying about below to gather breakfast which they carried out with a will. The home was tidied and put straight, breakfast cleared and tidied away before they were ready to set off. The boys were impatient to leave, but Mrs T had no intention of leaving an untidy home, not even for a day, and, of course, with people under her claws and getting in her way, she took longer than ever.

"There," she said finally, "I think that is everything ready. I hope you know the way, and don't fly too quickly. I'm not as young as I used to be."

"All right boys," chirped Mr Twitcherly, "out on to the branch and wait for us there."

The day was bright and promised to be warm, but because it was still spring it would not be too warm; ideal, in fact, for travelling. The boys hopped about quite impatiently again on the branch, picking up the odd insect, which they weren't supposed to eat because they gave them upset stomachs, and generally trying to hurry the day along. It was actually still quite early; about six o'clock of the humans' time but quite late by birds' standards. There was nobody around, except for the milkman who had been up and busy for nearly as long as the Twitcherlys, and who was just as happy, whistling along every driveway and path.

Mr and Mrs T eventually came out on to the branch to the excitement of the two boys.

"We're ready now," said Mrs T. "Boys! Come along; don't just sit there. Have you secured the door, father? We don't want any robbers to come in whilst we are away."

They set off finally, amidst much excitement and twittering of the boys. Thankfully the direction they needed to take to Mr T's cousin's home did not take them across that horrid wood, and Mr T was careful not to stray into the territory of that sparrow hawk. It just wouldn't do to have the holiday interrupted in such a way, let alone to end up on a hawk's breakfast table.

The sky was clear and the sun was becoming nicely warm. The larks had been active for a long time singing their enchanting songs and acting as the countryside's alarm clocks. The fields below bustled with a profusion of wildlife, and it seemed that every other bird that had hatched and was still alive had decided to take a late spring holiday at the same time. Initially, the boys had flown frantically in all directions, chasing each other and generally playing games, but after an hour or so they had settled down to concentrate on their flying and so remained close to their parents.

The country was pleasantly open for a change, with a gentle breeze breathing just enough to ruffle tail feathers and the new leaves on the trees. The farmers' fields, mainly around the towns, with their straight hedgerows and planted order, had long since disappeared, to be replaced by a picture of green rolling fields, random trees, woods, and meandering, silver rivers. There were so many places Furtive and Fearless would have liked to explore that their heads buzzed with anticipation.

Mrs Twitcherly flew closer to her husband and requested that they take a rest. "I think it's time we had a rest and a cup of tea," she gasped, a little out of breath. "I need to have a sit down and a break from all this flapping."

"There's a large elm tree just ahead," he replied. "We'll make for that. I'll flap on a bit and tell the boys."

When he had spoken to the boys, they all made for the elm, with its great spreading branches and cool shade. Elms had the reputation amongst sparrows of being very comfortable, and so they settled on one of the lower branches for a short while. The boys were ready to be off at any time, but Mrs T was firm that they should stay and be still whilst she had her rest and cup of tea from the flask they had brought.

The tree itself was on its own but was not very far from a small copse of birch and young beech trees. That small wood was very dense and dark, and although Furtive wanted to explore, the others said no. "You never know what's in such a place," said his mother in between sips of tea and nibbles of a digestive biscuit. "Besides, this tree is nice and comfortable and safe, and we can see if anything tries to get to us."

At that point, which seemed as good a point as any, Fearless turned to stretch his feathers and came beak to face with a ... cat! What a surprise and fright he had! But he recovered from his fright quickly enough to screech a warning to the others, and to fly into the cat's face and peck its nose. It was then the cat's turn to have a surprise and fright. In the face of what the cat thought was a very large, tough and aggressive bird of prey, the cat turned tail and fled. In the meantime, the others had instinctively flown on to a very much higher and slenderer branch (well, it was more of a twig really) to safety, and to see what was happening.

The cat had, in fact, been rummaging about in the leaves at the bottom of the tree, having crept out of the wood on silent paws to find food. It wasn't really a wild cat, just a rather stupid domestic cat that had lost its way and wandered further and further away from its home. It had tried repeatedly to find the correct way, but every time it had taken the wrong turning or someone had given it the wrong directions. So, up to now it had decided to stay in the wood.

With Fearless's attack, it had taken fright, jumped down from the branch (which wasn't really all that high anyway) and kept on running. Actually, Fearless had done it a good turn, for it set off running in the right direction for once, and didn't stop until it had reached its proper home.

Mrs T sat on the higher branch and shed tears of joy to see her wonderful son being so brave, and saving them from certain ... (well, she didn't really like to mention the word). Fearless joined them on the upper level, with his chest feathers puffed out in a show of pride, a feeling which was echoed by all the others. They spent a few moments more talking about the incident and recovering from the excitement before setting off again. This time they should manage to reach their destination with no other stop.

They travelled for ten minutes or so, and the weather changed for the better as they flew. It became cloudy, and whilst it remained warm, the sun was no longer beating down on their backs. Flying was much more comfortable for everyone. The land changed quite considerably too, the further away from home they were. The flat, green fields became rounded, undulating moorland carpeted with heather and bracken. They had never seen this sort of land before, and they flew more slowly with their beaks and eyes open in amazement. Very few trees gave definition and height to the smooth undulations, but there were lots of short bushes, mainly gorse and hawthorn.

"Is that the place, dad?" Furtive shouted in uncontrolled excitement as he dropped back to his parents. The area he had indicated was about a mile ahead, off to their left. It was quite a large wood, with a sheet of water off to one side.

"Yes it is," replied Mr Twitcherly. "Everyone make for the end of the wood nearest to the water. There you'll find the large elm I was telling you about. There are lots of branches higher up we can land on."

The boys shot off as quickly as they could, leaving their parents to come along at their own pace. The wind was freshening and blowing the few clouds across the sky quickly, and the air had developed a distinct nip. When they did arrive finally, the boys were already waiting on a large, flattened knotty branch in front of a rather grand door with a brass knob in the middle. This door was the height of two sparrows and the width of three, and was very highly polished. Obviously this was the residence of some wealthy and worthy person who must have high standing in the neighbourhood. In front of the door there was a wide, flat area which had been smoothed out and flattened, making the ideal threshold, on either side of which was fixed a gleaming and shining, curved brass banister, to provide support for anyone who might call.

Furtive and Fearless had not knocked on the door, because, not knowing Great Uncle Ebeneezer and having been brought up very well not to knock on unfamiliar doors, they knew to wait for their parents.

"My goodness!" gasped Mrs Twitcherly as she collected herself and straightened her feathers after her flight. "What a marvellous mansion this is! I have never been here before."

"No," replied her husband; "it's a long time since I was last here too, and that was before we met."

With that, he knocked, very politely, on the polished door, but there was hardly any sound at all, the wood was so thick. He knocked again, louder this time. Again, there was hardly any sound. In desperation, he grasped hold of the door knob and gave it an almighty tug. It came away from the door so unexpectedly that it took Mr T completely by surprise and he reeled backwards almost falling from the branch. There was a loud ringing somewhere in the bowels of the tree, and it was only then that they noticed a slender wire attaching the knob to the door. It served as two things, you see; if you pulled it, it became a door bell, and if you turned it, it opened the door.

Mr T replaced the knob, and they all waited. Nothing happened at first, but soon they could hear the faint sound of feathers rustling and a heavy wheezing coming nearer.

"All right! All right!" came a rather out-of-breath, gruff voice from the other side of the door. "No need to pull the door down. I'm coming."

The door opened slowly to reveal a rather large, stout sparrow with a pair of half-moon spectacles perched on the end of his beak. He was dressed in a flowing purple robe and had a round pill-box hat nestling precariously on the top of his head, with a yellow tassel hanging down the side.

"Well?" he said abruptly. "What do you want? I'm not expecting anyone"

"It's me, Great Uncle. Don't you recognise me?" asked Mr T.

The old sparrow shuffled over to the newcomers and had a good look at Mr T. After a few minutes, he stepped back with

Great Uncle Ebeneezer

a huge grin on his face. "Well, blast me britches and sizzle me socks!" he guffawed. "If it isn't my young nephew from the back o' beyond. I am glad to see you. And this would be your family? I heard from a passing jackdaw friend of the family that you had got yourself married ... and two fine sons! Well, bless me!"

They all stood there for a few moments without speaking, then the old sparrow burst in again as if coming out of a dream. "Well, bless me if I'm not forgetting my manners; won't you come in?" he bellowed. "Better still, seeing as you are down in this area, won't you stay with me for a while? There's plenty of room for you all, and so much to do."

"Well, that's what we ..." began Mr T but was cut short by a dig in the ribs by his wife's wing "... call very generous" he added somewhat winded. He had been going to say that that's what they had come for, but his wife had decided it would be impolite.

Old Ebeneezer led the way down into his home which was uncommonly large and very well-furnished. The door was on a spring so it simply closed itself, as Furtive found almost to his cost when he snatched his tail feathers inside only just in time. The entrance hall was wide and carpeted with down and small cork chippings fastened together in some invisible way. The staircase, off to the right as you went in, was also wide (it had to be to take Uncle Ebeneezer's ample frame) and turned as it ascended, like a spiral. The hallway and the other rooms beyond were all very well lit, but Furtive couldn't quite make out how. There were lots of doorways in the hall leading away to other rooms, but the one that they all went through was very well used, and it led into the sitting room.

"Find a seat! Find a seat! Make yourselves at home,"wheezed the old bird."Now, where did I put those spectacles?"He hunted and rummaged around until he found them on the floor, where, in fact, he'd dropped them only seconds before. He picked them up and absent-mindedly placed them on a small table stand by the fireplace. He sat down finally in a large armchair by the same fireplace. There wasn't a fire, of course, because it was still quite warm in the house.

"Tell me, my boy," Ebeneezer asked; "what brings you down to this part of the world? You're not thinking of moving are you?"

"No, Uncle," replied Mr T, "we came to visit you actually. I thought that it had been a long time - too long - since I had seen you, so I brought the family too."

"Glad to see you; glad to see you,"Ebeneezer butted in."You must stay a while - have I asked you that yet? - and sample our type of hospitality. Those boys are a credit to you and it's a pleasure to meet your dear lady wife. Was there much bother on the journey down?"

You will have noticed, of course, that Old Ebeneezer tended rather to change from one subject of conversation to another very rapidly. This made the listener very confused, trying to answer one question whilst listening to two or three others. The boys, although looking as if they were listening, were silently making their own plans for their stay.

After half an hour or so of trying to understand Ebeneezer's questions let alone answer them, they were all shown to their various rooms. One thing had been decided; that was that they should stay for one week. A week was long enough to do most things and see what you wanted to see, but was not long enough to over-stay your welcome.

There were five rooms upstairs of the same size with exceedingly comfortable nest-beds in each, and the rooms had the magic of being exactly what you wanted them to be. As soon as you walked in, it was as if the room had read your mind and made itself as you wished. Mr and Mrs T's room was warm and very comfortable, with all the things they had often wished they had at home; a window to look out onto the country, a firm but comfortable nest-bed, and a comfortably carpeted floor. The room taken by Furtive and Fearless was a mixture of the two; adventurous furniture, rush mats, and untidy nest-beds made from grasses, twigs and leaves, but lined with soft down. They felt as if they had lived there all their lives.

Lunch was at two-thirty prompt, and, as Uncle Ebeneezer had nobody else living with him, the Twitcherlys were amazed at the spread he had found for them - from somewhere. It was then that Furtive began to think there was more to Uncle Ebeneezer than met the eye (if it was possible with such a large frame as his!), and he decided to find out more as soon as he was able.

A table had also been conjured up from nowhere it seemed, and they all sat down to eat their fill. Half an hour later, when they had eaten to bursting, there still seemed to be as much on the table as when they had sat down. They had eaten so much, in fact, that they all felt very sleepy, and, what with the exertions of the journey and all, they sank into a lovely, warm and comfortable doze (the sort you like when you toast your toes in front of a winter fire after that rather large Sunday tea). When they woke, after what seemed like only a few minutes, the table was no longer there, nor was there any sign of the meal they had just eaten. Had it not been for the feeling of fullness in their stomachs, they would not have believed they had eaten at all. There was no sign of Uncle Ebeneezer either.

They waited for a short time, but when he did not return, they decided to go and do their own things. Mr and Mrs Twitcherly climbed rather slowly to their room to straighten a few things, and the boys of course took the opportunity to explore outside.

Chapter Five

Bedtime was always a strangely fraught affair, with Fearless and Furtive never too keen on wasting their time by going to sleep. There were much more interesting and important things to do and see. They would put off the inevitable for as long as they were allowed, with "I'll just finish off this ..." or "In a few moments ..." or "Please can I stay just ...?" Mr and Mrs T were almost always quite exhausted by the time they had managed to direct their offspring to bed (and to sleep). Somehow they didn't seem to need very much sleep, and despite their late bedtimes, they were usually up before the larks (who were not actually very early risers anyway).

This time, there were no problems at all, even though they were thoroughly enjoying themselves outside, doing what they liked most - exploring. It needed only one chirp from their mother to bring them swooping to the elm. She was agreeably surprised at their response and good behaviour. Perhaps, she thought, they wanted to go to bed in good time so that it would be morning sooner. After taking leave of their uncle, the family wound their way up the spiral stairway, and found themselves in their rooms before they knew it. One moment they were at the top of the stairs, and the next, the room was there, around them.

"Do you think Uncle Ebeneezer is an ordinary sparrow?" asked Fearless.

"No," replied Furtive, "he's different. I think there's something magical about him, and I intend to find out what."

Both sat down on their beds, straightened their feathers, and lay back. As they did so, the room started, very gently, to move, and eyes began to close. No sooner had these things begun to happen than morning surrounded them. They didn't seem to have been in bed for more than a few seconds, but they felt wide awake, restored and ready to go.

Their parents, on the other hand, had rested and slept for a very long time in their own extremely comfortable room. In fact, it seemed like they had been asleep for days; the longest they had known for a very long time. When they awoke, it was a nice, long leisurely awakening; no sharp, sudden jolting back to harsh reality by offspring or alarm.

Breakfast was taken in their rooms, and it wasn't until later in the day that the boys and their parents realised again that Uncle Ebeneezer was, in fact, alone and couldn't have served them all himself ... Anyway, there they were, by the sides of the beds on one of those small but useful wicker bedside tables which are very strong and have a reasonable lip around the edge of the top to stop marmalade from finding its way onto the floor, or to keep that extra piece of toast from getting lost under the eiderdown. Again, no sooner had the boys seen their breakfast than it was gone, and they were ready to be through that door and out into the nearby forest. It was one of those dull days, with a lot of grey cloud which seemed to threaten rain if you stepped out of the door. Nonetheless, it was perfect for exploring and rummaging about in exciting places.

"Let's have a look around the lake today," said Fearless. "It looks as if it could be quite interesting."

"Yes, and then the wood," replied Furtive. "There are lots of trees I have never seen before."

Once agreed, they didn't even need to go out of the door; they were there, gliding over the water towards the far shore. You might have guessed by now that Uncle Ebeneezer was no ordinary sparrow, nor was his house an ordinary house. He was, in fact, a magical sparrow, and there was a magical spell over the whole of his house. Whatever was required was done, and whatever anyone inside needed or wanted, was provided. You see, Great Uncle Ebeneezer was very old indeed; in fact, he was so old that nobody knew when he had been born, and nobody could remember a time when he wasn't there.

He wasn't really their great uncle, but seeing as nobody knew what he was, and he was a relative, it seemed like it was a good enough name. His great age was one of the reasons why he was so absent-minded on some occasions about his own possessions; yet he never forgot anything about others. He knew the names of all the trees, all the other birds and animals, what the weather was a year ago, and what it would be like the day after tomorrow. In fact, you might say he knew everything.

"This is a wonderful house, Uncle," said Mr T as they came into the lounge. "It's a constant source of wonder and surprise. Our own home is decidedly plain in comparison."

"Yours is an oak, is it not?" the old sparrow asked, and then answered, "Yes, it is. Too hard, oaks are. Not enough comfort.

Now, you take my elm ..." and with that, he launched into how wonderful elm trees are for home-building, and how they should change from their own oak. Whilst this was going on, Mr and Mrs T had made themselves very comfortable in the great winged fireside chairs, and they had decided they would not move until they had to, or something happened to make them.

Meanwhile, outside, the two boys were soaring, swooping and gliding over the water, just like the fishing birds they had seen the day before. They were trying to catch some of the small silvery fish they could see just beneath the surface of the lake. What they would have done with them if they had caught them, they had no idea.

When they had made several passes over the water, they became a little tired, and decided to explore. On the furthest bank there was an enormous sand bank, and in it there were many holes of roughly the same size, big enough to let a sparrow through. These were the old nest holes of a colony of sand martins from the year before. They had, alas, not returned to them to take up residence again this year, and so they had fallen largely into disrepair, and some had become dangerous. This proved too appealing for Fearless, and he made straight for them. Furtive followed, of course, not wishing to be thought a chicken, but he wasn't too happy about the situation at all.

"We shall explore," Fearless stated without any sign of wariness. "They might be full of treasure. I have heard tales of sand martins hoarding lots of things we might find useful."

Sand martins' old nesting holes

"I don't know really, "answered Furtive, rather unsure and wary of anything he was not sure of. "They look terribly dangerous to me. Besides, we didn't ought to stray too far away from Uncle Ebeneezer's house; we might be needed ... for ... something ..." His voice trailed to almost a whisper. In fact, he was quite frightened at the prospect of entering any of the holes, but he wasn't going to say so whilst Fearless could hear. His favourite pastime was rooting about where he could see and where things were relatively safe. It was very unlikely a tree would fall on your head, but an old sandy hole was a different matter.

Furtive's last words were not heard by Fearless who disappeared into one of the largest holes he could see. Furtive sidled up to the hole his brother had chosen, and very cautiously peered around the edge into the darkness beyond. He could hear the faint chirping of his brother along with the occasional cough and sneeze caused by dust he had disturbed.

Outside the sun was beginning to rise over the woods behind him, and its warming rays gently stroked the feathers on Furtive's back. He moved slightly away from the entrance to the hole, and turned around to watch the various types of duck on the lake. The mallard, in their blues and greens, were out in great numbers, as were the coot and moorhen, with their black suits and white and red nose pieces (Furtive didn't know which were which). There were quite a few gulls lazily bobbing up and down like white corks on the gentle ripples, because they weren't too far from the coast, and often gulls came inland to feed, always preferring to take an easy lunch.

He was thinking what a marvellous thing it must be to be able to swim and dive like the ducks and that he should really get around to learning one day, when his attention was jolted back to the holes by a deep rumble and a muffled shout. He was overcome by a terrific fit of coughing as a great cloud of sand and dust shot out of the hole, completely covering him. When the dust had cleared and he had shaken it out of his feathers, he poked his head into the hole.

"Hello ..." he shouted. "Are you all right?"

There was no answer.

He shouted again. "Can you hear me?"

Silence.

Where there had been an echo, as in a large empty room, the sound was now muffled and dead. Furtive strained with all his might to try to hear any sound at all from his brother, and then he didn't know what to do.

"I know," he shouted in something of a panic, "Uncle Ebeneezer will know what to do."

"What seems to be the trouble, my boy?" came the familiar wheeze from nearby Furtive's right wing. "Are you having a spot of bother?"

It was Great Uncle Ebeneezer.

"But ... How ....?" stuttered the amazed little sparrow.

"Where's your brother?" interrupted the old bird. "Gone into the old workings, has he? I always said they should have been demolished long ago. Danger to life and limb. Never mind, we shall have him out of there in a twinkling. Can't leave him there. Shan't be long."

As he was talking, he moved a little closer to Furtive, and peered at the bank. The sides began, very slowly at first, to move, and then more perceptively to crumble. Then finally, without any sound at all, the sand fell away and disappeared, leaving one rather dusty little sparrow floating in mid-air, seemingly asleep. Furtive had watched the whole process with wide astonished eyes, and when he saw his brother floating there, his beak sagged so much it nearly hit the floor! Fearless woke up eventually with such a violent sneeze it sent him crashing to the ground.

"What on earth is the matter with you?" he said to Furtive, picking himself up from the floor and flapping over to his brother, knocking the sand out of his feathers, eyes and beak as he waddled. "How did I get out of there? The last thing I remember was falling asleep and having an odd little dream. Then - air and sunshine!"

"It was Uncle ..." he eventually blurted out, turning round to see ... nothing! "He was here, I'm sure," he mumbled to himself. "I think he was, anyway."

There was no sign of anyone other than the two sparrows, a flock of passing geese returning after the winter, and half-a-dozen collared doves sitting cooing in one of the birch trees of the wood.

"As I said before," said Furtive coming to himself again, "the safest place is in that wood, and that's where I'm going. You can follow if you wish." With that, he flapped into the air and made for the nearest trees. Fearless didn't follow. He'd had enough for one morning, and he decided to fly across to the small wooded island in the lake, and have a rest until lunchtime.

The outer trees of the wood were very inviting, shady and cool, which was a welcome relief for Furtive as he didn't like too much of the warm sun on his back. He landed on one of the upper branches of a rowan, a tall, stately small-leafed tree with a few bright red wizened berries still remaining from autumn. Here he paused for a while to look around and decide where to explore first.

There were so many places that he couldn't possibly cover them all in a day. So he decided to map the wood and explore one patch of it each day. This was not quite as difficult as it might have at first seemed, for the wood was divided naturally into distinct areas; lots of short shrubs and bushes together, growing outwards to blanket the bottoms of the tree boles; there were places where the tree trunks almost touched each other, they were so close together.

The place he liked best and which he decided to try first was a strange mixture. Bushes mingled with trees quite haphazardly, and many different types of creeper wound their way around them, sewing them together with enormous blanket stitches. The wood wasn't quite as easy to fly in as he had at first thought. For one thing, branches did have a habit of getting in the way, which made you have to dodge and flit rather quickly. If you weren't careful, at best you would lose direction, and at worst you would wrap yourself around an unbending sycamore. Furtive, therefore, had to be extremely careful.

What also surprised him in this wood was a thing that at first had not been obvious, what with the novelty and excitement. There were no other birds to be seen.

"Strange," he thought. "Still, no interruptions from nosy busybodies."

So, with that, he swooped down to the first area of Exploration Furtive.

Some of the bushes on closer examination were similar to the ones he had seen before in gardens, but not exactly the same, and others he had never seen before. Some of them were so aromatic that they made him cough, and others had a great number of fine lacy leaves which tickled his beak and made him sneeze. But this did not last for long as he became more used to his surroundings. The outside world was completely forgotten as he burrowed his way through tiny gaps in twig and leaf, and wriggled past tall and short stems alike. The sun stole through the leaves in only a few places, but this didn't worry Furtive at all. He was completely at home now, really in his element. He couldn't see why so many people were afraid of dark woods. He wasn't.

Suddenly, he stopped and pricked up his ears. What was that? Some sort of a ... no; must have been the breeze. He carried on examining a rather strange depression under a small privet-like bush. There it was again! This time it was definitely not the wind. It sounded very much like a creak followed by a bang.

"What could that be?" thought Furtive, his eyes searching backwards and forwards in the gloom. He didn't really want to be caught unawares, and, although he preferred to be on his own usually, this was one of the rare times when he would have liked some company.

He moved out gingerly from under the privet bush and peered forward, trying to see through the darkness. Silence descended again.

He was on the point of turning around when the noise occurred again, nearly making him jump out of his feathers. Part of him - the sensible part - told him to turn around and leave as quickly as he could, but the other part was a fearless explorer (or so it said), and told him to go on. Not wanting to admit he was afraid, he took up his courage in both wings, and sailed forth. In fact, he didn't sail but picked his way very carefully and quietly through tangled briar and bramble, under a very large, flat juniper, over and through a flowering currant bush (minus flowers), and up to what must have been an extremely old and thick yew hedge. The needles and branches of this hedge swept the floor right the way along its length, and they were so close together that even an inquisitive sparrow could not find its way through. As far as Furtive was concerned, this was merely a detail, and he would find a way through!

Fears forgotten, he scrabbled along the hedge in search of an opening, and, finding only half of one, he pushed, wriggled and squeezed until he was through. On the other side, he stood panting for a few seconds, with his feathers ruffled and untidy from his efforts. When he'd had time to catch his breath again, he looked around and simply stood in amazement at what he saw.

He was standing at the edge of an enormously long and wide stretch of grass which could only be described as a lawn. It seemed to have been well-tended and looked after as if it had been cut only the day before, and must have been about half the size of a football field.

It was still dark around because along each side there were four enormous oak trees whose branches were so long and high up that their leaves interwove above forming a leafy roof over the lawn, and through which very little light came. It was light enough, however, to see where the noise was coming from. At one end of the lawn, looking quite eerie in the gloom, and shining slightly, was a house.

It was a large house with white painted walls, with five windows and a door facing outwards. The noise was coming from the door which was open and swinging freely in the slight breeze. It resembled the houses on Mulberry Road in many respects, but, of course, they were proper houses in a proper road, not like this one, stuck here in the middle of nowhere.

'Why is there a house in the middle of a wood,' thought the little sparrow. 'And a house which could be lived in?' This latter thought struck him quite forcibly when he'd had the time to let it sink in.

The house in the wood

"People!" he twittered. "There must be people."

You see, he was a very logical sparrow, and could work out that if the house and grass had been tended, it couldn't have been done by anyone other than a person. He had heard strange stories of very odd people from his parents and from others older than him, so he would definitely not be visiting today. He would, like the good sparrow he was, be going straight back to his Great Uncle Ebeneezer's house for lunch, if it was still lunchtime. But all the while he found himself being drawn nearer to the house. He was a house sparrow when all said and done, so why shouldn't he visit, really? This being drawn was not only desire on his part. Even if he had not wanted to go there, he would not have been able to do anything about it; he was compelled physically, by some unknown and unseen power.

Furtive quite cheerily hopped and sidled along the lawn, nearer to the house with every step. Every so often he would stop momentarily and look around him, to see that all was safe. He needn't have done this, for he knew there was nothing else anywhere around. Even the breeze had stopped rustling the leaves and banging the door of the house. Was everything waiting for him? He became a little nervous the nearer to the house he came. It seemed so large; much larger than those he was used to in Mulberry Road, and very different, he now decided.

He reached the house eventually, with much detouring, wandering about, and hesitating. The walls were textured with a gravelly, stippled effect, and were off-white, which seemed to glow slightly in the half-light. The downstairs windows were shuttered, but those upstairs were only half-curtained, having a gap of a few inches between drapes.

"Just a quick hop up there to see what it's like inside," he muttered to himself, and with that he fluttered up to the eves above the first floor rooms. Passing by the first batch of windows he threw a quick glance through the chink in one of the curtains, and was so amazed at what he saw that he almost flew into the eves above him. He managed, however, to collect himself and to scramble up on to the guttering above. There he sat, somewhat out of breath, and more than a little shaken by his encounter with the wall and by what he thought he had seen through the window. So, before jumping to conclusions, he decided that the best thing to do was to have a brief rest and regain his strength, and then to go down to have another look.

"Dear, dear!" he muttered. "It shouldn't be ... Well, here goes."

Taking a deep breath, he dropped from the guttering, and then, when he came to the window in question, he tried to hover like he had seen other birds do. He did manage to do this for a few moments, just enough time to confirm what he had in fact seen before, before he glided again to the lawn below.

The room he had seen was a large one with no visible door, and it was bare of all furniture, except for a very large, fine-meshed cage which fitted exactly inside the room. Inside the cage there were miniature plants, trees and shrubs of all kinds, set out like a small wood. Running through the wood and into a small clearing just in front of it was a stream, or perhaps on that scale it might have been described as a river. It seemed as if someone had taken part of the British countryside, shrunk it, and set it in this room.

The most surprising and amazing thing about this whole piece, however, was that there were miniature animals and birds in that wood; small by human standards, but Furtive could make out what they were, even though he'd had only a quick glance. He couldn't understand, however, how or why such things had been done, so he decided to try the other two windows on the first floor. It was very much easier with the other two, for the centre one had a nice wide window sill, and the other one had a large branch hanging just in front of it.

At the second window, Furtive perched on the sill and bounced in towards the glass. This room was even more surprising than the one before, for this time there were tropical palms, mountains running down to a large flat sea, and in that sea there were fish, whales and porpoises; all things which Furtive had never seen and didn't know the names of.

Then he flew along to the third window, expecting to find something even more wonderful and exciting, but on alighting on the branch in front of the window, he was a little disappointed. In this room he could see only another wood, but different this time, for by the wood was a small lake, and around and about there were many gorse and hawthorn bushes; at the head of the lake there was a large elm tree. Half way up that elm tree, he could see a door with a big brass knob in the middle, and a curving brass banister on either side ...

Furtive, being an intelligent bird, realised quickly what he was seeing, and almost fell off the branch backwards. Quickly he pulled himself together and shot off at great speed towards the hedge. His desire to get away from this place as quickly as possible blotted out all other thoughts.

Nearing the hedge, to reduce flying time, he decided to try the impossible - to fly over it! It loomed before him, seeming to be twice as high as when he came in, and just managed to squeeze, at speed, between the hedge top and the overhanging branches of the nearby trees. Instead of scrambling, squeezing and scurrying amongst the bushes, brambles and briar, he flew into the first tree and worked himself to its top, where, on breaking through, he was half-dazzled, half-blinded by the brilliance of the day. Actually, the day was quite dull, but Furtive had become so used to the darkness in the wood. Up at the top of the tree he felt a keen but refreshing breeze, enough to aid his flight home, well, to his Uncle Ebeneezer's anyway. He launched himself into the wind and headed for the elm.

The distance wasn't very great so he arrived quite quickly. Rounding the last batch of trees, he was surprised to see the elm and the lake still there! In no time at all, he was landing on the branch outside Uncle Ebeneezer's front door. The interior of a house had never been so inviting or so welcoming ...

"Well, young-fellow-me-lad," snorted Uncle Ebeneezer as Furtive poured himself through the open door. "You're too late for lunch. We ate ages ago, but I have no doubt that we could conjure up something for you. Come in, into the sitting room, and I'll have a tray made ready as we go in."

"But … Uncle … the wood!" Furtive tried to butt in.

"Ah, yes; the wood," he said slowly. "So, you've been there, and I take it you saw … the house? And what was inside?"

"Yes!" Furtive answered, "but how did you know?"

"I know a good deal, my boy," Ebeneezer replied, looking over his spectacles.

They went into the lounge, where a large fire burned in the grate. Ebeneezer beckoned him to one of the huge, winged fireside chairs, and they both sat for a few moments in silence. It wasn't until they had been sitting there for a while that Furtive noticed a large tray on a small table beside him just off to the right. He wasn't sure it had been there when they went in, and Uncle Ebeneezer hadn't moved in that time, neither had anyone come in. Still, there was a good spread of choice delights to soothe his excitement.

"Tuck in, my boy," encouraged the old sparrow. "We will talk as you eat."

"I shall tell you of times past, and the way things were and are, and shall be," he started. "I shall not tell you all, because if I did you would still be here as the autumn leaves became covered by the winter snows."

"Many, many years ago, before the lake at our door grew from its stream, and when the wood was but a part of its present size, there came to live a man and his wife. They seemed a happy couple, and they built a house in amongst a large semi-circle of trees. They laid out a fine big garden of lawns and many plants and shrubs, all enclosed by a large yew hedge. There were such shrubs as gave a great deal of pleasure to the birds around in spring, and a plentiful supply of berries, seeds and fruit in the later parts of the year.

"Over the years the garden matured and grew, and expanded, but the family didn't seem to change much. Eventually, a little boy came on the scene. He grew rapidly, and enjoyed the excitement of roaming and exploring, rather like you, my boy. After a while he became bored with the countryside he had explored so often, and instead he became enthralled with his father's work. Now, the boy's father was a collector; not of small items like a rabbit's paw, dried holly berries, or odd pieces of string, like anybody else. No; he collected items like trees, rivers, and mountains ..."

"But," interrupted Furtive through a mouthful of bran bread and butter, "how could he collect those things? They're too large."

"... and all sorts of other items," Ebeneezer went on. "You see, he was a shrinker. He would decide on what he wanted, and he would shrink it to whatever size he needed to fit the item into his collection. He not only shrinks - yes, I say shrinks, because he is still here, though nobody has seen him for a long time - objects, but he has been known to reduce animals, birds, and ... people. What you saw in those rooms exists now only in his collection, and where they once were, are now empty spaces."

"But ..." blurted out Furtive again, to be cut short this time.

"The one you saw which isn't part of the collection was the tree and lake - this tree and lake,"went on Uncle Ebeneezer."As long as I am here, it will never be part of that collection. He has tried many times and would dearly like to succeed, but so far we have held out."

Furtive sat there with wide, wondering eyes. He knew his uncle was magical, but just how great he hadn't realised.

"Where have you been?"came a voice from the hall doorway. It was Mr Twitcherly, with Mrs T and Fearless just behind.

"He has been here with me," said Uncle Ebeneezer with a wink to Furtive."We have been having a chat."

Furtive knew from then that this was to be their secret, known only to them.

"Oh, that's all right then,"said Mrs T."You must be ready for your tea, missing your lunch like that. I think it must be about time."

Furtive looked at Uncle Ebeneezer who smiled slightly and winked again, though no-one else saw, and glanced quietly round at the tray. But, of course, you have guessed; it wasn't there. Anyway, he was a growing sparrow and could have eaten his next meal quite easily; besides, hadn't he had a very busy, tiring and strenuous day?

After tea they were all content to spend the rest of the evening quietly in the sitting room, with Uncle Ebeneezer telling many of his interesting and exciting stories. Furtive half-listened and half had his mind on what had happened during the afternoon.

Bedtime was not very late that night, as everyone was tired enough after a busy day.

Chapter Six

The remaining days of their week's holiday passed very quickly and pleasantly, with no other real excitement. Uncle Ebeneezer very often took them on rambles and excursions into the countryside, and to places no one else could have known about.

The last day came, as last days will, and then it was time to leave. Although they had had a wonderful time, they felt inside that it would be nice to be back home again.

"It has been wonderful having you here," said Uncle Ebeneezer as they all stood in the hallway. "You must come again soon, but I expect you will be wanting to get back to your own home now." He always had the knack of saying what they were thinking and putting people at their ease. "The journey I know is a long and tiring one, so take great care."

With that, they all thanked him for his hospitality and kindness, and, with a last look over their shoulder at the elm, they flew off. They circled the lake and headed off in the direction of their home. They had been going for what seemed like only fifteen minutes or so, with the prospect of a long flight ahead, when Fearless dropped back level with his parents.

"Aren't they the chimneys and television aerials of the road near to our home?" Fearless asked, clearly puzzled.

He was, in fact, correct. They had somehow come home very much more quickly than they ought to have. They couldn't remember anything about the journey, only that they were nearly home. They were all extremely puzzled - except of course for Furtive. He knew why, as, I expect, you do.

They approached Mulberry Road from the same direction as that used by Mr Twitcherly when returning from his fateful visit to his cousin. He was very wary as they approached, remembering his experience of only the other week, but there was no hawk about.

It was early evening as they turned into Mulberry Road, and so was just at that time when it was neither full day light nor yet dusk. They could see perfectly well, but it was obvious it would soon be dark.

The lights were beginning to appear at odd windows here and there up the road, and as they crossed the street and landed on the chimney pot for a rest before homing in on their oak, they were greeted by the friendly and welcoming sound of Juniper, coming up from his bowl in the back garden. It was good to be back, even though they had enjoyed their break. They all happily flew down to the branch. Mr and Mrs Twitcherly landed and hopped perkily around to their front door, to be greeted not by their door at all, but a rough-looking chunk of wood. The Ts looked at each other, puzzled and not able to understand.

"We are at the correct address?" twittered Mrs T. "I know things can get a little muddled, especially in this light."

"Yes, my dear, we are not mistaken," replied Mr Twitcherly quite deliberately. "I could find our home in the dark. Besides, we have the only oak of this size in this road."

He hopped up to the piece of wood and tapped on the side.

"Anybody in there?" he chirped.

Silence.

He knocked louder with his beak, but not being a woodpecker, he only developed a headache.

"That's it!" he shouted. "What we need is a woodpecker. I will pop round to Lemuel, our much esteemed neighbour, and see if he will help. You three stay here." With that, he hurried around to Lemuel's front door, knocked three times, and, surprisingly, on the third, he opened the door and invited Mr T to come in.

"No thank you," he replied politely. "We were wondering if you would kindly give us your valuable time, and lend us some assistance (Sparrows always spoke like that when they were being formally polite). We've only just come back from holiday, you see, and there seems to be something blocking our doorway. We wondered if you would give us a hand to remove it."

"But of course my dear chap," replied Lemuel, "only too pleased to help a friend in need. As my old mother used to say ..."

"It is rather urgent," Mr T butted in.

"Oh yes, of course," said Lemuel. "There I go chattering on again when there's work to be done. We'll go this minute."

They set off again around the tree, and joined the rest of the family.

"We have heard muffled scufflings inside," said Mrs Twitcherly, "but nothing much really. There has still been no movement of the lump of wood."

"We'll soon alter that," said Lemuel. "Did I tell you that I specialise in the removal of unwanted pieces of wood?"

With that he started drumming on the outer side of the blockage. He stopped every so often to give a progress report (which the sparrows could see anyway).

"This wood is quite soft," he reported, "and we should be through in no time at all."

His drummed away with his sharp beak, making several holes around the outside edge of the wood so that the centre could be moved easily. He was just starting to drill the last hole but one when there was a distinct movement to be seen on the wood. He saw this, but as soon as he stopped, the movement also stopped.

"Only one thing to do," he said, "and that is to carry on regardless."

The movement this time became more obvious, and the more Lemuel drilled, the more the plug of wood moved out. After only a short while more, the plug came out of the doorway with a resounding pop, like the cork springing out of a gigantic bottle. This, of course, caught Lemuel, and the sparrows for that matter, very much off balance, and sent them bowling backwards, beak over tail, on top of one another. They remained in a tangled heap for some moments, and when they were able to pick themselves up again, they noticed a large bushy tail blocking their doorway.

They all stood there, beaks agape, except for Fearless of course, who darted in straight away and gave the intruder, whatever it was, a sharp peck on the rear quarters. This, naturally, prompted swift action, and the tail disappeared, to be replaced by a small head and whiskers. It was a squirrel. It gave Fearless a very cross look and rubbed its hindmost parts with short stubby paws.

Encounter with a squirrel

"What's the meaning of this?" it squeaked in rather a high, thin voice which sounded like a door hinge needing oil. "How dare you disturb a fellow in his own home and then attack him in such a vicious manner!"

"I beg your pardon ...!" started Mr Twitcherly.

"I will not give it! And even if I wanted to, I wouldn't give it to you!" it interrupted.

"... but this is not your home!" went on Mr T, completely ignoring the squirrel's attempt at repartee.

"It's our home," butted in Mrs T, "and we have lived here for a long time, and you are not required, and we should be obliged if you would pack and leave."

"No fear!" returned the squirrel. "This is my home and I will defend it to the death."

Lemuel, all this time, had stood back not wishing to interfere in business which was not really his, but now stepped forward, not wishing his friends and neighbours turned out of their home. He marched up to the squirrel resolutely, and gave him an almighty peck on the knee.

"All right! All right!" he squeaked. "You win; I'm going. I can't fight two at once." With that, he tucked his tail under his arm, turned, and scurried down the tree and out along the lawn.

Juniper had been watching the proceedings all this time with interest from his tub, and had been waiting for just such an opportunity as this. He sprang into life, across the flower beds, and caught the squirrel a glancing blow across the back. This new terror added steam to the squirrel's legs, and he shot off behind the garage with the cat in hot pursuit. That squirrel was never seen in that area again. Juniper came back a few moments later, smoothing his whiskers with his paws as he glided slowly back to his resting place, a smile of satisfaction flicking across his face.

"Well now; that's a turn up for the book," said Lemuel scratching his head with his claw, "and here was me thinking all was well. He was so quiet, too."

"We had better go in and inspect the damage," said Mr T.

They all filed through the doorway and into the main living area. There wasn't much mess really, except for nut shells and acorn cups which littered the floor, and a rather musty smell as if the house had been shut up for weeks. The other rooms hadn't been touched, and the front door, they found, had been pushed wide open and wedged back against the inside of the outer wall, with no damage to it at all.

"Well, fortunately," sighed Mrs Twitcherly, "there's nothing done here which can not be put right quickly. We will just straighten things, and then have some refreshment."

"Will you stay, Lemuel?" asked Mr T.

"No, thank you very much," he replied. "I really must get back and finish the work I have started. I'm widening the fourth vertical passage to the left. Either it has shrunk or I have grown since I first cut it out."

He said his goodbyes, and skipped around to his place. The day was now disappearing very rapidly; the lights were all on at Number 18, and David could be seen at his bedroom window. He had watched the activity with interest and enjoyment.

"Well, they're back again," he said with a smile creeping across his face. He turned out the light once he had made sure that there was no more to see, and went down stairs. Much as he liked all the other wildlife which visited his garden, he preferred the sparrows.

Chapter Seven

It passed to that warm time of year when, apart from a short period early in the morning, all you wanted to do was to sit in the shade of some large and dense tree sipping something cool. Summer had finally arrived amidst a great rush of insect activity. In fact, there were so many insects in the air that the house martins were busy catching them from dawn till dusk. Except for in the cooler parts of the day, Mr and Mrs Twitcherly ventured out very little. However, Furtive and Fearless had the time of their lives.

Fearless was the sun-loving member of the family, staying outside in the blazing sun from first light until its red rim sank below the edges of the house tops. This was the time of year he loved the most!

Furtive, however, couldn't stand the heat for too long, but he didn't mind because there was a great profusion of shrubbery and plants which gave excellent cover and cool, soothing shade. Here, amongst the red-hot pokers, azaleas, rhododendrons and montbretias, he would root and search to his heart's content, coming out only for food or when shadows were long enough over the lawn to provide shelter from the heat.

Even Juniper, who usually enjoyed summer basking in the warmth and comfort of his tub, found the temperatures too much as the summer wore on. He would often be found following the shade around the garden as the sun moved; by the garage, by the shed, and most of all, in the late afternoon, by the back fence, under the cypress tree. There, he had a good vantage point from a slight rise in the ground just under the lower branches. He had made an indentation in the mound and had lined it with dry grass and fallen cypress needles, and, as the garden sloped naturally towards the house, he could see well all that went on. For him this was not the time of year for chasing or fighting; it was the time for dozing comfortably between meals.

The days drew on, and still the sun blazed unabated in an azure blue sky. No clouds could be seen, not even the smallest cotton wool ball! At first both people and animals had thought that it was nice to have such lovely weather, but as the time passed and water grew scarcer, everyone began to think that perhaps it wasn't such a good idea after all. The first to suffer were not the birds, as they had kind souls who put out water for them, but it was the plants! As watering bans came into force, they began to wilt, and eventually to die, and as always it was the deepest rooting plants and trees that survived the longest.

David, the boy at the house, had by now had his fifth birthday. That day had been a magnificent affair, with lots of his friends bringing presents. They had tea out on the patio (organised by his mother, of course), and played games and had races and prizes afterwards on the lawn (organised by his father this time).

They had had about an hour's worth of games, as many could not stand to be out in the heat for too much longer, so, to everyone's relief, they continued with quiet games inside. All the birds had stayed well out of the way, except to watch for a short time from the safety of the trees. Not all little boys were as good with the birds and animals as David. They, I am sure, would have lain hold of the sparrows, if they had been able to catch them. They didn't understand.

Juniper also took part in the games, but ended up limping back to his tub when some clumsy child stepped on his tail, which thrust a screech from his throat and brought tears to his eyes. When they had all gone, the sparrows emerged again to continue with their business. All, that is, except for Furtive; he was under the goatsbeard which was by now drooping rather alarmingly, and in fact had been there for most of the day. The children had not ventured as far as his hiding place, and he, of course, took no notice of them as they had not disturbed him.

Throughout the drought so far, for drought it had been officially declared, David had been faithful to his friends. He had refilled the bird bath (even though he shouldn't have) every time it mysteriously became empty. He had suspected that the one with the great "thirst" was Mr Black, the resident blackbird, who would sit, hop and flap in the water, making him the cleanest in the area! He had also brought them food to the table as many times a day as they needed it, and he never ceased to enjoy their antics. The birds for miles around had heard of his generosity, and lots came to see for themselves (and to eat and drink, of course), but almost invariably the regulars had been there first and scoffed the lot.

On one particular day, Furtive decided to do something different. He remembered it well because that was the day he woke up in complete darkness and thought the sun had forgotten to rise. In fact, Fearless's tail feathers had fallen across his eyes. So, in the early morning coolness, before the sun had had chance to hot up, he bade "au revoir" to his parents (he had once learned that from a French sparrow who had lost his way on a return journey from some relatives in the north), and flew off over the house tops in search of excitement (his father had said afterwards that it was most unlike him to go off like that, and he put it down to too much sun). It happened to be a Saturday in the human world (every day was much the same in the sparrow world), and so all around was peaceful and quiet. There were no noisy cars setting off, no loud disturbances from children going out to school, and no shrill alarm clocks making a nuisance.

He glided down from the chimney and, on swooping over the large privet hedge, his eye was drawn to something new in the front garden. It was quite tall, mainly thin, and had a large flat piece at the top, and was red and blue. It was the colours which drew his gaze. He executed a very smart turn on his tail, and, dipping back, he landed on the flat piece. Twisting, and hanging almost upside-down, he tried to see what it was all about.

There was writing on the front in big bold letters, but never having studied such things, he didn't understand what it said.

However, thinking that it had to be something very important, he flew off, deciding to tell his parents later if the opportunity arose. For now, he was away on a jaunt, to enjoy himself. He thought he might fly down to the other end of Mulberry Road in search of new grounds and perhaps new friends.

This was the first time, apart from their holidays, that Furtive had been away from his home tree, and as he flew further down Mulberry Road, his eyes opened wider with amazement. The houses became larger, and the gardens were not only larger but had many more trees, shrubs and plants. There were several with large ponds with lots of green floating plants, and some with fountains (which were allowed to work only if they used the same, re-circulated water), and others, much bigger, which were landscaped to look as if they had a mountain stream cascading through them. He was so amazed at what he saw that he almost forgot to flap his wings as he passed. He decided to inspect what he saw more closely, so he picked out the grandest house he could see, with the best looking garden (the most trees and shrubs) and flew in to have a rest.

He chose a very stately elm tree with a magnificent umbrella of spreading branches. This tree would have dominated the garden of Number 18, but here there were many others similar; oak, rowan, birch, and others Furtive did not know. The sun was beginning to stoke up the air again, so he hopped in along a particularly large branch to find a nice cool shady part where he could sit and rest and look around.

The garden he saw stretched out below him like a small park. The central feature, of course, was the lawn, which, despite the drought, still looked amazingly green and healthy. There were several horse-shoe island beds of roses in the lawn, and one enormously wide and long herbaceous border. The back border was almost too far away to see, but he could just make out some of his very favourite trees. At the other side of the garden there was a triple garage. Behind the garage stood a beautiful cedar and glass summer chalet (almost as big as an ordinary house), and with a great barn of a potting shed close by it.

The most amazing thing of all was the rockery behind the chalet. It had been built obviously to look like a mountain stream, and as such, it was very successful. It resembled a fast-flowing course in every detail - boulders (miniature, of course) strewn here and there, stretches of rapid with small waterfalls, quietly eddying backwaters, and all along, spume and spray. Along the banks of the stream there was quite an extensive, miniature pine forest. You would have been forgiven for thinking you were in the mountains looking down at some stretch of country as yet untouched by humans.

The gentle bubbling and chuckling of the stream was interrupted, and blotted out by a tremendous squawking and twittering in the undergrowth at the foot of the lawn. Furtive's feathers stood on end in anticipation of what was happening. He left cover and flitted from tree to tree until he came within sight of the disturbance. He sat (on the shady side) at the end of a huge overhanging branch and craned his neck to try to see what was happening. The noise stopped suddenly, and Furtive saw a huge ginger tom cat pad out of the shrubbery and on to the lawn. Something seemed different about it; different from any other cat. Furtive, being quite a perceptive creature, saw almost immediately what it was. Out of the side of its mouth there was a feathery tail, and from the other hung a beaked head.

"Golly!" Furtive twittered. "It's another sparrow."

Without really thinking about the consequences, he launched himself from the branch and down at the cat. All he could think about was rescuing a fellow sparrow, stranger or not. He landed fairly and squarely on top of the cat's head, who was very surprised indeed to have such an unexpected lodger. Once there, he commenced to try to bore a hole between the cat's ears to let it know he was displeased. This had the effect of making the cat's jaw gape open in amazement, giving the other sparrow chance to escape, which it took with both wings. Rather cross at losing its lunch, the cat swished its paw over its head in an attempt to catch the interloper.

Furtive wasn't being quite as vigilant as he might have been, and was caught a glancing blow across the back, sending him flying through the air in an almost never-ending summersault. He ended up at the base of a gorse bush where his feathers became entangled in the crossing branches. The cat gave a screech of triumph and lurched forward.

Furtive was not yet finished, however. When the cat pounced, the sparrow summoned all his strength, pulled back his head, and, as the feckless feline was about to snap, Furtive shot his head forward again and caught the cat fully on the nose with his closed beak with as much force as a small woodpecker. This was too much for the cat; first banged on the head, and then stabbed in the nose, he slunk off, tail between his legs.

Strange cat with sparrow (Patience) in it's mouth

When it had disappeared around a flowering currant bush and was out of sight, the rescued sparrow fluttered down to see what it could do to help.

"Can you manage?" she enquired. Yes, indeed, it was a girl sparrow, and there was nobody more surprised than Furtive to see her there. Most others would have been long gone.

"Yes ... I ... think so ..." grunted Furtive, removing his feathers from the branch one by one. "Just one ... there, that's it."

"I think you are very brave, and I thank you very much for rescuing me," she blurted out in one breath, quite embarrassed by it all. "I do hope you are not too hurt on my account."

"No, not really," he went on, shuffling his claws a little. "Just a little stiff around the primaries, that's all. Nice place you've got here. Your garden?"

"I live here," she answered, "in that elm over there." She indicated an enormous tree which must have been hundreds of years old, and which would have quite dwarfed Furtive's home. "Would you like to come back and meet my parents?"

"Er, well, I ..." he stammered. "Yes please, I would."

She gave a chirp of pleasure, and flew into a nearby beech to await Furtive. He joined her after straightening his feathers (you can't really go visiting with ruffled feathers, can you?), and they flew together towards the elm further down the garden.

The entrance was approached by a winding stairway leading from a broad landing space on a high branch. The door was made from highly polished oak, with a large brass knob to one side. Also, there was a small, semi-circular window at the top of the

door, with darkened glass, shaped like the slices of a cake. She
pulled a large knot at the side of the door, and a chiming bell rang
somewhere inside, and at the same time the door began to open
itself. This surprised Furtive, for he thought that the only magical
tree was that belonging to his Great Uncle Ebeneezer. There
was no one in the large hallway at all, for he had already looked
behind the open door. The hall was wide and well-carpeted with
down and small cork chippings fastened together in some weird
and wonderful way. The staircase, off to the right as you went in,
was also wide, and turned as it went up, rather like a spiral, and
Furtive had a very strange feeling that he had been here before
(which, of course, was impossible!). There were lots of doorways
in the hall leading off to lots of rooms, but the one she took him
through was very well-used and led into the sitting room. This
room also was familiar. As he looked around, he noticed someone
occupying one of the large winged fireside chairs. On hearing the
newcomer, the figure stood up to face them both.

"Uncle Ebeneezer!" gasped Furtive. "But I ..." The figure was
in fact the very image of the old bird they had visited some time
before.

"Not quite, my boy," he wheezed, with a smile. "We are alike,
and so I know a good deal about you already."

The girl sparrow, who was called Patience, expressed a little
surprise until the old bird explained to her. Then she told her
story to him whilst he listened quietly and with interest. He was,
in fact, Patience's father. "Could he be related to old Ebeneezer?"
thought the little sparrow, trying to account for the similarity of
house and the magical quality Furtive felt.

"Mother's out visiting at the moment," Patience's father said with his wing around his daughter (she was their only child), "but it won't be long until she is back to meet you. I really can't thank you enough for saving my little chick. You must be a very brave youngster to do what you did."

Here, Furtive became very embarrassed, and it was a good job he had feathers on his face or else they would have seen him blushing. "Don't mention it" and "It was nothing really" was all he could muster in answer.

As by now it had reached just past mid-morning, the old bird thought it only polite to ask Furtive to take a spot of tea and a little sustenance with them. As Furtive was a little peckish from his exertions, he agreed readily. The sitting room was very similar to the one in Uncle Ebeneezer's elm except that he thought the fireplace seemed bigger (if that was possible). Furtive was so absorbed looking around at the objects in the room and wishing that he had a room like it, that he didn't notice the appearance of a small but heavily laden table. He was sure that Old Benjamin (for that was his name) had not moved since he had last spoken to him, but he couldn't be altogether sure. Things in the room seemed to be quiet and still, and yet there was a feeling of life in them, a feeling that anything could move around should it so wish.

"Come on then, my boy," chirped Old Benjamin, "Tuck in. You'll have to keep up your strength if you want to carry on rescuing people and all that. Lived here long? - Pass the seed cake, Patience my dear if you please - but of course, I know how long you've been here; how silly of me. Just forgetting; for the moment, I thought you were as old as me."

The conversation (one-sided, of course) lapsed for a moment or two whilst they all took beakfuls of cake. Furtive thought that he had never tasted such delicious cake.

"Yes, it is good, isn't it!" Benjamin said when he had emptied his beak, as if answering Furtive's unspoken words. His eyes looked at the old bird rather suspiciously and with more than a little wonder. 'Could he read thoughts?' Furtive wondered. There was, however, no reply to that, as Benjamin had finished his refreshment and was looking out of the window at the side of the room. Again, Furtive had not seen him move, even though he had been looking at him for nearly all the time. The tea things were removed, not by magic this time, but by Patience, who said she would be back shortly. Furtive had lost all sense of time (which wasn't too difficult for him), and as far as he knew, it could have been late afternoon (which it was, actually).

"Well, my boy," Benjamin started again, "will you come and visit us again?"

"Yes, please," said Furtive politely. It wasn't, however, the usual politeness which means "thank you for asking" but is never taken up. He meant it genuinely, and it was a genuine question from Benjamin.

"Well, in that case," he returned, "you shall come again; just whenever you have a mind. All you have to do is think of us, and you will be here. Well, goodbye, then, my boy."

With that, Furtive found himself outside, at the top of the stairway to the outside door. He hadn't quite understood Benjamin's meaning, but he didn't dwell on it. Patience was

Benjamin's Elm

beside him. She must have anticipated the puzzled look on his face for she tried to explain.

"Father is a very wise old bird," she began. "I don't understand everything he does, so I should just accept what he says if I were you. He won't let you come to any harm. Shall we see you again?"

"Yes, if you'll allow me," he replied, getting ready to take his leave. "Must be off now. Bye."

Her 'goodbye' carried up to him, as he took off, borne aloft by a slight but welcome breeze. He noticed as he winged his way home, that there were a few clouds in the sky, one of which, small in size, was blotting out the sun. The breeze was blowing the way Furtive wanted to go, so he had good help on the way. When he reached the house he remembered the large blue and red thing in the front garden, so he went to have another look.

It was a little different this time, but again he couldn't make it out, so he shrugged his feathers and glided over the roof and down to his own home.

His mother was glad to see him as he fluttered in through the doorway, as he had been away for most of the day. The Oak wasn't as grand as the other he had seen, but to him it was home.

Chapter Eight

The drought ended suddenly and very dramatically. Furtive had gone in and decided his stomach felt that it was time for something to eat. He had sat down to his tea with the others when Mr T noticed something strange.

"Dark out now," he observed, standing by the door. "That's very strange at this time of the afternoon and ..."

His words were lost in a great rolling boom outside.

"What's that?" snapped Mrs T sharply, taken by surprise and made more than a little frightened. "Sounds like the end of the world!"

"Not quite, my dear," Mr T replied, trying to soothe her nerves; those nerves he had been acquainted with for many years. "We are in for a storm by the looks of it." His form was silhouetted against the door as a bright flash of lightening gashed the sky. The attendant clap of thunder was so severe that the tree shook to its very roots, sending the family off-balance, and rattling the furniture inside.

"Are we safe here?" she gasped rather shaken.

"Safe as oak trees my dear," came the swiftly reassuring answer. "We've absolutely nothing to worry about." He didn't actually feel all that steady himself but it wouldn't have done to have shown it. He knew how upset his wife became over matters such as this, and the last thunder clap hadn't done anything to make things better. The storm was directly overhead, with lightening winning the race over thunder by only a split second.

"Here comes the rain," Fearless added as large globes of thunder rain began to bounce from everything within their sight. The blackness deepened to be split only by the intense brightness of the lightening. The four sparrows were standing a little way from the open door, with their beaks gaping at the incredible sight. None of them had seen such a storm; the boys had experienced no more than a slight shower previously. Within a few moments, a continuous sheet of water was cascading onto the once-parched earth, and where there was once dry, dusty ground, now was becoming a sea of black watery mud. Plants and quite large shrubs were battered into submission as if by some enormous trampling foot.

The noise about them was quite terrifying and almost continuous. Mrs T was becoming more agitated as time passed, when without warning they were all knocked to the floor by a tremendous rolling boom. The doorway became blocked by twig and leaf, some of which covered Mr T.

"The tree's been struck!" shouted Fearless above the noise, and he dived under the leaves to pull out his parents. Mrs T was shaken but not hurt. Mr T had not been so lucky. He had received a glancing blow to the side of the head and had been knocked unconscious. There was a slight trickle of blood from a cut above the bridge of the beak but otherwise he seemed to be all right.

"Is he ...? Is he ...?" she asked, nerves in a knot, wanting to know.

"No, mother," came the reassuring reply from Furtive, "just knocked out. I should think he will be quite normal as soon as he comes round."

The two boys carried his prostrate body in to the nest area, and laid him down to recover naturally. The storm raged outside, unabated, and by now the garden below was completely awash, with water flowing under the fence at the back. The Twitcherlys were very lucky to have their shelter and safety, if only just; much luckier than many other animals which were caught on the ground. During this commotion, Lemuel the Woodpecker slept peacefully and deeply. He swore quite definitely that he had heard not the slightest sound and couldn't for the life of him understand next day where all the water had come from.

"Someone must have left a tap on somewhere," was his muttered explanation, as he returned to his excavations.

Mr T also slept the night away, and only regained consciousness the following morning in time for breakfast. This morning was as fair as any so far experienced by the sparrows. The storm had put everything into its giant washing machine and next morning had hung it out to dry in the brilliant warming rays of the sun. Steam soon began to rise from the fence, paths and rooftops as the sun touched them with its fiery fingers. The drops of water, hanging from branch and twig, never reached the ground; they simply evaporated in mid-fall.

By the time Mr T had awoken from his enforced sleep, Furtive and Fearless had removed all trace of the branches that had caused the damage to their father, and were in process of straightening outside, and repairing the hurt caused to their landing strip and door. Many of the great branches of their tree had been torn out of their sockets and thrown down on to the garden, causing a great deal of damage to fence and plants.

"I'm absolutely starving," noted Mr Twitcherly, "and my poor old head hurts."

"You're lucky, you know," twittered his wife, "not to have had your feathers permanently bent with that branch. You gave me such a turn! I thought we had lost you for good, but you've got the boys to thank for your safety and ..." She would have carried on for another hour had not the boys entered, laden with tasty morsels for their father's breakfast (and for their own of course!). David had not forgotten them even after such a battering from the weather; bird food, bread, and bacon rinds he had managed to provide for his birds, all of which were Mr Twitcherly's favourites.

"I think we can say now with certainty that the wretched hot weather is over," Mr T spluttered through a mouthful of wholemeal bread - nothing but the best - "and can look forward to proper weather for a change. Well," he went on after finishing his repast, "that was indeed splendid, and I think I must get up and ..." He flopped down again with a bump, with his eyes spinning and his head throbbing - a reaction from his accident. He wasn't, after all, quite as youthful and sprightly as he would have liked to think.

"You must rest there for a while longer, husband," Mrs T ordered. "You're not as young as you used to be."

"But, I ..." he protested, his face feathers colouring bright red.

"No buts," she went on, "you can get up when I say for a change."

No change at all then, thought Mr T, for she always said, and decided, and thought.

"Steady, steady," she chided Furtive as he skidded in from the landing strip, which they had cleaned up too well, obviously.

"But Mother! Father!" he twittered in excitement. "Come see! There's a big thing at the front of the house, and it's eating up all the people's things!"

"What on earth are you talking about?" Mr T interrupted, holding his head. "Take it steadily and explain."

"Well," he started again, "it's as big as the house - or nearly - and the back is open, and there are people putting things from the house into it, and ... and ..."

"Let's go and have a look," sighed his father. "Where's your brother?"

"He's sitting on the roof, keeping watch," Furtive answered, hopping from their landing strip in a perfect take-off. Mr Twitcherly's take-off wasn't quite as spectacular, but just as effective. Furtive was very surprised when he neared the roof top to see his father already waiting, next to Fearless, watching the antics.

"Well Dad," Furtive chirped as he came into land, dislodging a small piece of chimney pot, "wasn't I right?"

Mr T remained in silence for a few moments, watching the antics below with interest and a half smile on his beak. Furtive was becoming restless by this time waiting for his parents' much esteemed approval and agreement.

"'Fraid not my boy," Mr T added as the television and two fireside chairs were 'gobbled' up by the monster. "That's a removal van, I'm very much afraid. The people are moving house ..."

" ...But how can you move a house?" chipped in Fearless. "It's much too heavy, and it doesn't have wings!"

"No! No!" laughed Mr T. "They can't move the house itself. They are moving to another one. Somewhere else."

"But why?" Fearless interrupted again, scratching his head. "There are enough crumbs and worms for everyone in the garden."

"Perhaps they're moving to a better house, or are wanting a bigger garden," was the reply from their father, who turned to Furtive to explain further about "monsters" and removal vans, but Furtive's mind was elsewhere. All that talk of removing and large gardens had whisked his thoughts back to that strange house in Uncle Ebeneezer's wood ... The other thing to occupy his thoughts these days was sparrow-shaped and answered to the name of Patience.

Now, she was the sort of sparrow who didn't say very much, but tended to pop into the mind at all sorts of odd times when you were least expecting it, and Furtive was beginning to have a liking for her - as a friend, of course! Besides, he now had the run of her father's house, being able to explore at will. That house was the sort of place which kind of "grew" on the mind too; the more you explored and found, the less you realised you had seen, and the more you wanted to see. It was rather like a maze, but a maze with a difference; all the rooms (and there were many) always amazingly led back to the sitting room! This puzzled Furtive greatly, as did the fact that wherever you were in the house, if you wished to be back in the sitting room, there you were straight away, in a cosy armchair, with a tray of food beside you.

However, the introduction of new events, like the removal of the human family, was very short-lived, and his mind returned ever to his two main interests.

"... and I'm sorry to see the little boy go," came the final word from father. "Aren't you, my boy?"

"Er, yes. I think so," was Furtive's flustered reply.

"You're not with us today, are you?" Mr Twitcherly said quietly. "Something on your mind, eh? Perhaps it's ..."

He didn't have time to finish as Furtive blushed to the roots of his feathers, for two other things happened at the same time. Fearless had been perching on the small television aerial, and, unknown to him, the wires had almost rusted away (they were not the modern non-rust ones we have today, you see); so that when he decided to do a few acrobatics across the antennae, the wires finally parted. Fearless regained his balance and flew over to the others on the roof's ridge tiles, but the last they saw of the aerial was a spectacular gyrating somersault off the edge of the roof into the garden below, with a trail of shattered slates behind, watched by a small crowd of gaping on-lookers. At the same time, a jet aeroplane decided to fly a very low pass over them at great speed; the air from its passing nearly pulling the sparrows from their perch. The sound wave from the plane crept upon them, and when it arrived, its intensity nearly deafened them, shattering the windows in the house as it exploded.

This was too much for both families; the sparrows very hurriedly decided it was time they weren't there, it being too dangerous a place for them; the humans buried their heads in their hands in despair to see their property being damaged.

Fearless and their father made their way back to the tree, but Furtive felt the need for something else; something exciting and different. By now his wings knew the way to Old Benjamin's abode without Furtive having to think, and so he was almost there before he had really decided to go.

He was surprised to note that their garden didn't seem to have suffered at all from the storm. There were no signs of excess water, no broken branches; in fact, nothing to suggest that this was anything other than a perfectly normal unexcessive summer day.

"Hello young fellow," came a voice from his left as he came in to land in front of the polished door. Furtive turned around, beak open ready to speak, to find ... no-one! Puzzled, and slightly ruffled, he reached out for the bell-pull.

"The door's open; go on in," came the voice again, this time from just behind his right ear. He spun round expecting to find someone there this time, but no luck. Ready to take off again, he was suddenly held in his place, and even drawn towards the door which had begun to open gradually as he approached. He was unable to resist, and as he crossed the threshold, there came a slightly wicked chuckle away in the sitting room. Still puzzled, Furtive crept on claw points towards that room, to be greeted by the ample form of Old Benjamin; or was it Ebeneezer?

"You'll have to pardon my little joke, my boy," the old sparrow broke in; "just one of the whims of an old bird." The old pill-box hat, tassel and half-moon spectacles were exactly the same as they were the last time Furtive had seen them.

"But that was ..." stammered the young sparrow.

"...what you call magic, I think," chuckled the old sparrow. "Anyway, welcome. I'm glad you could call again. Patience will be so pleased when she gets back from her aunt's home just around the next corner and four houses down."

"I was only thinking the other day ..." went on Furtive.

"Yes, it is rather like old Ebeneezer's place," butted in Benjamin with a twinkle behind his glasses.

"But ... but ..." stammered Furtive, making it a habit. "I hadn't said ... I was just ..."

"...thinking it!" Old Benjamin interrupted once more. "Same thing. So sorry, old chap; force of habit, you know, reading other people's minds. You liked Ebeneezer's abode, didn't you?" he continued, looking over the top of his spectacles rather like a wise old professor talking to a student.

"Rather!" Furtive enthused, forgetting his surprise. "It was quite ..."

"... unusual?" smiled Benjamin, finishing his sentence for him again. This is rather an infuriating habit when you are about to finish a conversation, and someone does it for you; but you couldn't be annoyed with the old sparrow. So Furtive simply accepted it as part of his makeup.

"Peckish, my boy?" queried Benjamin from his great winged armchair by the fire. As Furtive nodded, he wondered why it was that whatever the time of year, there was always an open fire in the grate; and what was more puzzling was that the temperature in that room was never more nor less than just right and comfortable. Whilst he was daydreaming, the old bird's voice jolted him back to reality; jolted him back so much that Furtive started, turned towards his host, and nearly knocked over the tray which was standing on a small mahogany table next to his chair. That tray wasn't there before, thought the young sparrow. Or was it?

The happenings in this tree puzzled him as much as those in his uncle's tree. In fact, was this his uncle's...? No, it couldn't be! The two old birds were completely different ... weren't they? He noticed a slight twinkle in the old chap's eye; or could it have been a trick of the light reflecting on Benjamin's spectacles?

The snack (which was more like a feast) was just right; seed, wholemeal bread (with honey, what's more!), a variety of other tasty morsels, and a large jug of milk for him to sink his beak into. By the time he had finished, he was full to bursting, and yet there didn't seem to be any difference in the size of the tray! All the while, Benjamin had been talking; about this and that, the winter that had been and the summer to come. Throughout his tales there was woven a thread of mystery and excitement, with mutterings and mumblings about the forest and the deserted house; time and again he returned to this subject.

That room was cosily warm, and Furtive was comfortable in his armchair before the fire. His eyes slowly became fixed and focused on one brightly burning log which had assumed the shape of a large barred window. His gaze was drawn ever nearer to that window as the rest of the room faded, darkened and disappeared. That window filled his whole mind, so that his head began to swim with the intensity of his concentration on it.

Suddenly, his head cleared, but instead of the comfortable surroundings of the sitting room, he found he was sitting on a branch in a very dim wood, with faint sun rays stabbing the gloom every so often. Behind him he could just make out a great stretch of well-manicured lawn, arched over by the branches from enormous oaks. Before him was a bare window in a frighteningly large house; bare, that is, but for a series of thin iron bars, meshed together by criss-crossing wire.

Chapter Nine

Panic took hold of the little sparrow! Even though at times he felt grown up, he was still very small compared with this enormous house and forest. He had no idea where he was, or why he had come here. The feathers on the back of his neck began to bristle with fear. His beak became dry, and his throat began to seize up. He flicked his head from side to side, hoping to find a friendly face, but none appeared. He was completely alone!

What to do? Nothing for it but to take courage in both wings, to find where he was. As he hopped tentatively a little nearer to the window and the cage inside it, something clicked in his brain. He realised that he'd been here before! It was the wood near Uncle Ebeneezer's home tree!

His first reaction was to fly up to the top of the tallest tree and set his bearings for the old bird's home. However, as he was about to do just that, some of that daring and courage he found on his last visit, began to course through his little body. Brave little sparrow that he was, he would explore, as he had been dreaming about and threatening to do for some time now.

All around was quiet. In fact, the silence was so deep, it threatened to envelop him. Every move he made, every rustle of feather against feather was a raging storm; every step became a deafening creaking and groaning; every breath rushed from his beak like a passing flock of geese.

He became aware gradually, as he approached the pane, that there was another sound. Very subdued it was, like … like the distant crashing of waves on a sea shore. Probably insects on the move, thought Furtive. By the time he had hopped onto the window sill, he could hear the pounding of his own heart, beating time to the other noise.

The inside of the room was quite indistinct because of the reflection of the slanting sunbeams and the closeness of the mesh forming the cage. However, one corner of the window had a crack across it, leaving a triangle of glass quite loose, which when pushed in, would leave a space large enough for an inquisitive little sparrow to squeeze through without too much damage to feathers.

That task duly carried out, one little beak very tentatively pushed through one entrance to adventure. First the beak, then the eyes, then the whole head inched their way through, and still the sparrow couldn't see too clearly. The tail finally gave a slight twitch and disappeared.

Furtive nosed around the side alcove of the window, but didn't get any further. He stood, motionless, rather like one of those rusted weather vanes on an old church tower, with his eyes goggling and beak agape at what he saw. There wasn't time to see anything else! There was a flash and the sound of a high wind, and all that was left by the window was a swirl of downy feathers chasing each other around the sill. Furtive could no longer be seen!

He had never been in a whirlwind before; for that's what seemed to have taken hold of him. It was as if he had been caught in a blinding whirl of snow blizzards, but without the settling flakes or icy cold. There was no noise except for the pounding of blood in his temples, and the knocking of his knees with fear of the unknown.

The white fuzziness stopped suddenly, to be replaced by a distant crashing and swishing noise, gradually increasing in volume. Where had he heard that sound before? Could it have been...?

A brilliant, almost blinding light was switched on. There were a few wispy white clouds in the sky, a slight breeze to ruffle his feathers, and a branch under his claws. He was back in the tree, thank heaven!

He was about to launch himself to soar aloft in an attempt to take his bearings when he realised that the branch he was sitting on was rather strange and different from the one outside the window. This was no oak branch, but had large leaves with many slender fingers; and those round fruits were not acorns but ... but ... coconuts? But how...? Very swiftly he jerked his head, in something of a panic, over towards the source of that noise he had heard, which had now grown to be quite deafening. It was then he realised what it was ... the surf pounding a deserted beach!

The almost-white sand glinted under the unrelenting glare of an intensely bright sun, which recalled painful memories of the extreme summer they had only just managed to survive. Only, this sun was far hotter than anything he had experienced before, and fortunately for him, the part of the branch he was perched upon was in the shade. Where on earth was he? His mind was wrenched back to the window.

On occasion, as the reader will no doubt have realised, Furtive was inclined to be a little slow to understand situations. He had found his way, of course, into that room, and the noise he had put down to insects, was, in fact, this surf pounding this beach.

Panic is a strange thing. The first, and only, thing to come into his mind at this time was Frobel Fleetfoot. How would he get his worms here, or any food for that matter? He didn't think that David, the little boy at the house, would have come too, to bring him food; so, what would he do?

'Forage, you dumb head!' a very firm and decisive voice from within his own head shouted. Of course! Why hadn't he thought of that himself? He, of all birds, knew about foraging; he did it all the time. But he would have to be very careful. You never knew what might be lurking in the undergrowth.

He was a little wary at first, but his natural curiosity (and hunger, I might add!) overcame his better judgement, and, casting aside all caution, he launched himself from his perch and zoomed through a small gap in the foliage, and landed on something ... soft and rounded. As he came in to land, amidst tangled leaves, grasses and tree roots, he heard a sharp hiss, somewhere to his left, as if someone had put a hole in a gas main. He turned to find the source of the noise, and nearly jumped out of his feathers seeing a very large flattened, chisel-shaped head staring at him through yellow, half-lidded, unblinking eyes. The swaying of this head atop a slender neck (which seemed to stretch for rather a long way), and the constant flickering of a forked tongue slightly mesmerised the little sparrow.

The gas leak grew louder as the swaying head came nearer. The fangs flashed as the jaws struck at ... nothing! Furtive was through a nearby hole and ten yards away by the time the snake was wondering why its throat was not now full of fat, tasty bird. The snake didn't like sparrows anyway - whatever they were!

Furtive took refuge on a high branch of a strangely misshapen tall shrub, shaking from beak to tail. He wasn't now so sure that this had been such a good idea after all. Dodging and escaping the attention of cats and sparrow hawks was one thing, but mobile gas pipes with deadly fangs and no sense of humour was something else.

"Who are you, then?" said a strange squawk close by his right ear, almost causing him to have a heart attack for the second time in as many minutes. He spun around on his heels, beak at the ready, to be confronted by a large green parrot. Furtive didn't, of course, know that it was a parrot, because he had never seen one before. He did realise eventually that it must be a distant relative because of its wings, feathers and beak. The accent, however, puzzled him.

"You're new here, aren't you?" the parrot continued in a broken screechy voice, with an accent that could only be described as foreign. "Where'd you come from? Don't know the place, do you? Craaa!"

"Do you always speak so quickly and ask so many questions?" retorted the little sparrow, somewhat irritated by the quizzing he was receiving. "I would have thought it might have been better to offer help and advice."

The green feather duster stepped back a pace, beak open slightly in surprise, and with narrowed lids, it eyed Furtive

Archie

warily. After a few moments of intense scrutiny, it let out a terrific squawk of glee, and hopped around from foot to foot as if the branch had suddenly become too hot.

"I like you! I like you!" it croaked, paused momentarily, and then continued without stopping for breath; "haven't seen anyone like you for such a long time. What's your name? Mine's so long it would take ages to tell it. My friends call me Archie."

Furtive was about to reply when he was interrupted by a deafening roar and a tremendous crashing in the undergrowth.

"Oh, oh!" cut in Archie. "We'd better be off a bit higher up. Sounds like trouble coming our way."

He rose into the air, what small amount there was contained in the slight space between trees, and beckoned to Furtive to follow. Their destination turned out to be the top-most branches of an enormous tree with small spiky leaves which prickled the feet. From their eyrie-like perch they could see quite well down into the clearings to right and left. Furtive felt a little dizzy and sick, for he had never been so high before without flying. The slight, pleasant breeze he had felt down below had grown up here, and it began to rock the flimsy twigs they were sitting on.

"Shouldn't be long now," observed the parrot, looking down into a reasonably-sized clearing. "Hear that snorting?"

The only thing the sparrow was able to make out was the slow thud, thud of several obviously very heavy feet on the hard earth.

As the thumping came nearer, the tree began to shake alarmingly, making poor Furtive more than a little afraid what might happen next. Suddenly, the tree shook violently again, taking Furtive completely by surprise. The animal below had blundered into the trunk at the base causing the slender branches above to twang like elastic bands, having a catastrophic effect on poor Furtive.

Not having expected anything so violent, he wasn't maintaining as firm a grip as he might, with the result that he was catapulted from his perch, past the surprised beak of his new-found but soon-to-be former friend. Archie wasn't, however, quite as slow as he looked, and as Furtive whizzed past his face, he shot out a claw and managed to halt the sparrow's headlong, powered flight with a timely tail-grapple. Archie put the sparrow down next to him, correct way up, minus a few tail feathers, but otherwise intact, and chuckled at his own dexterity and swift reaction.

"Craaa! Who's a pretty bird, then?" Archie crowed in triumph. "Archie saved the day! Archie saved the day!"

"Thank you very much," said Furtive politely, "but I wish you wouldn't talk so quickly. I can't keep up with you."

The parrot nodded, slapped Furtive on the back, and turned a neat summersault around the branch, still clutching the same with his claws.

"Where do we go from here?" asked Furtive. "I'm beginning to feel just a little hungry. Could you please show me the way out, back to the tree outside the window?"

"There's no way out ... 'cos we're here," squawked the parrot, cocking an eye and moving his great green head closer to the sparrow. "What's 'window', eh?" he went on with a quizzical look on his face. If you have ever seen a large green parrot with an enormously curving nut-cracker of a beak having a quizzical look on its face, you would know just how comical the whole picture appeared. Furtive, however, couldn't see anything even mildly amusing about his situation. The idea of being in this tropical paradise didn't have any appeal whatsoever for this very English suburban sparrow.

"Like, I mean, do you have worms in these parts?" Furtive went on, under the puzzled look of Archie the parrot.

"Don't know. Don't know," Archie replied. "They can't be very tasty - even if I knew what they were. Are they good to eat, eh? Nice and crunchy and sweet?"

Furtive could see that he wasn't going to get very far with this conversation, so he simply asked how to obtain food of any description. Hungry young sparrows had to be fed, or they wouldn't grow into strong healthy adults.

"Yes; course there's food, food. Plenty of it. Plenty," went on Archie like a gramophone with a sticky needle. Trouble was, you didn't know just where the needle was going to stick, so you couldn't close your ears. "Follow. Follow me!"

He took of in a spectacularly gyrating fashion, which amounted really to a clumsy back-flip, and disappeared through the foliage in a storm of leaves and bark. Furtive took off more efficiently and with less fuss, as quickly as he could so as not to become lost. After all, this bird was his meal-ticket, for a while yet at least.

It took Furtive fully five minutes to find Archie again, good forager though he was. Even so, it was only by following the harsh squawk Archie was so fond of uttering that Furtive was able to keep up. Not so sure, the little sparrow landed on a large, knotty and gnarled branch of some sort of tree he had not seen before (as was the case with all the others), and which no doubt had some equally unpronounceably long name. He poked first his tiny beak through the foliage, which was extremely dense, and then his head, to be met by a loud 'caw', making his neck feathers stand on end and him quiver in fright.

"Craaa! Craaa! (which must have been Archie's attempt at a laugh)."Caught you! Caught you! Craaa!" the parrot screeched, hopping about again with glee at his most excellent sense of humour. You will have realised, no doubt, that by now Furtive was becoming somewhat irritated and fed up with both the antics and the behaviour of his vividly-coloured cousin. However, he decided to bear with him a little longer in the hope of finding his way out (after he had eaten, naturally).

"Here you are! Here!" squawked the parrot in rather a muffled voice. "Food is what you wanted. Food ..."

"I know," sighed Furtive. "... is what you wanted."

"No! No!" hooted the parrot, doing a passable impersonation of an owl in flight. "Wrong! Wrong! He doesn't listen, does he? Food ... is what you shall have. There. Finished."

He offered the little sparrow a large, hard-looking object about the size of Furtive's head, still held in his great cracker-like jaw.

"But ... but ..." stammered the sparrow. "I can't eat that!" he went on, aghast, giving the nut (for nut it was) a tentative tap with his tiny and very puny beak.

"Why not? Why, eh?" asked the parrot, thrusting the object towards Furtive. "Good food. Nice and crunchy."

"It's too hard for my beak," protested Furtive. "Besides, how can I get inside? I'd need a woodpecker for that thing; do you know a woodpecker who would oblige?"

"Craaa! Gracious me, no. What's 'woodpecker'?" Archie quizzed. "Watch me! Watch out!"

With that he rolled his beak from side to side slightly, and pressed. Nothing happened. He hopped around a little, scratching his ear with a claw, and started again. After a few moments of sustained pressure, the outer shell of the nut began to show signs of stress, and suddenly the two halves parted company at speed, leaving a smaller, perfectly round 'middle' clamped firmly between the parrot's jaws.

"Try now, eh?" asked Archie, talking like a ventriloquist trying not to let his mouth move for fear of losing his morsel.

This time Furtive was determined to show he was no weakling, and he attacked the nut with the point of his beak (which sparrows are not supposed to do) with such force that it took the parrot unawares, sending him backwards, claws still grasping the branch, spinning like some clockwork pendulum gone haywire. Fortunately, he managed to right himself again, nut still in place, whereupon Furtive launched his second attack upon the elusive food. Great hunger and not a little desperation, lent urgency and strength to the bird.

Success is a mighty thing, and, with a slight squeak of triumph, Furtive shattered the nut very dextrously, catching most of the pieces in his eager beak. Although not quite to their usual taste, hungry sparrows, with neither worms nor crusts in the larder, tend not to be too choosy about what they eat. Six such nuts were cracked and dispatched, much to the intense amusement of the parrot and satisfaction of the sparrow.

"Well," said Furtive, licking his beak and smoothing away nut particles from his facial down, "that was, well, quite satisfying if a little unusual. Now, please, would you tell me the way out of this, this ... paradise?"

"No way out! None at all!" screeched the parrot. "Better make the best of it. What did you say you were called?"

"I'm a sparrow," answered Furtive, quite deliberately, puffing out his chest and pulling himself up to his full height.

"Pleased to meet you Sparrow," said Archie, spluttering over the last word with which he found great difficulty because of the curvature of his beak. "Follow me", and with that he launched himself into the air.

At the same time, several things happened. A large branch crashed through their cover, narrowly missing the two companions. Archie had risen only a few centimetres when he was knocked back to their perch by the wind from a tremendous wing-beat. A great shadow fell on them almost freezing them to the spot, and enormous talons reached out to pluck the two hapless creatures towards a gaping, cruelly curved beak.

The day would have been completely lost (along with their lives, of course) had it not been for the sparrow's agile brain and quick reactions. He grabbed Archie by his iridescent tail feathers and, borrowing super-sparrow strength from somewhere about, he heaved the terror-frozen parrot away only a split second before that awful, frightening scimitar of a beak scythed through the air where they had been but a moment earlier.

Still assuming Superbird stature, Furtive hauled the parrot through the foliage and down into the thicker parts of the tree, thereby preventing the bird of prey from following. Archie, by this time, had shaken off his fright and was now complaining bitterly at the pain in his rearmost parts.

In his haste to escape the flying executioner, Furtive had not really looked where he was going, and rushed headlong into a great black, cavernous expanse, cutting out all the light.

"Who on earth has turned out the lights?" was all the time he had to utter before the wicked jaws snapped shut on its first meal of the day. He opened his beak to screech for help - when he lost consciousness completely.

A violent earthquake had started, it seemed to his subconscious brain, with his little body being shaken to bits. He was sure that this was the end of all things, when a dense mass of white static electricity started up in his mind's eye. Surely heaven wasn't like this? And that smell of newly-resinous wood? Did they have elm trees up there?

"Come on, my boy," cut in a very familiar voice. "Come on. Time for you to wake up."

It was Uncle Ebeneezer. And this was his elm.

Oh, what joy!

"So I'm not to be eaten then!" was all he could utter with relief. "I must have dreamed what happened to me," he continued, scratching his head with his claw. He looked up at

Uncle Ebeneezer who said nothing, but had a slight hint of a smile on his beak. Furtive was glad it had been only a dream, and reached out with his other claw to take some of that most excellent seed cake his uncle always had handy. It was then that he noticed he was still clutching two rather large, bright green feathers...

Chapter Ten

"Well, my boy," Uncle Ebeneezer wheezed, "have you had an adventure or two?"

"I think so Uncle," Furtive replied slowly, whilst he was pushing bran bread and honey into his beak as fast as was polite with one claw, and scratching his head with the other. "You see, there was this ..."

"Tell you what; tell you what," butted in Ebeneezer; "haven't got much time now. You tuck in and I'll come back later. Got a few things which need some attention," and with that he disappeared through the doorway.

It was very pleasant in that room as ever, with a good log fire roaring in the grate, a comfortable armchair to relax in, and a tray of excellent food at the ready. Warm and comfortable and drowsy is how he felt. The fire crackled and the flames licked the chimney back, fixing Furtive's glazed eyes on their activity. Stomach full, he began to slip into that comfortable state of dozing which comes just before full sleep.

"Hello," came a sweet tinkling voice just by his right side, making him start rather violently, almost knocking over the tray in his surprise.

"I'm sorry," the voice continued, "I didn't mean to startle you." Furtive turned sharply around to see another sparrow standing behind. It was Patience.

His beak dropped. That comfortable state he enjoyed before had been driven out by shock and surprise.

"How did you get here?" he mumbled in disbelief.

"I live here of course," she replied with a gentle smile. "Don't you remember?"

"Yes … yes, of course," he muttered, still surprised. The tree was his Uncle Ebeneezer's. Or was it Benjamin's? They were completely indistinguishable; and either he had been mistaken before, or there was magic afoot.

"Father told me a few moments ago that you had come and were waiting," Patience went on. "I …"

"But …" interrupted Furtive, more than a little perplexed. "I was …"

"Having a snooze?" she interrupted. "I know. Anyway, shall we go out now? It's a beautiful day and …"

Days, weeks and months passed, and Furtive's visits became more and more frequent, until he was almost living at their home. Mr and Mrs Twitcherly had noticed both with satisfaction and regret that the day was fast approaching when their little fledgling would leave them to make a life of his own. Mrs T had many a weepy day (when all the family but her husband was out, of course), and it took him a lot of effort to comfort her.

"He'll come to visit us often, my dear," he would say to her. "I am sure. He'll have to live his own life some day, and if he's found a nice young sparrow to look after him and to share his life with, then so much the better."

This was the nature, more or less, of all the conversations they had had concerning the young sparrows.

"I think we'll pay a visit to my cousin-three-times-removed-on-my-mother's-side Finch," said Mr Twitcherly one bright cracking blue day quite unexpectedly."We haven't seen them for such a long time, you know my dear; and of course it will give you something else to do other than dwell on other matters." (Furtive's leaving home is what he meant, of course, but he didn't say so for fear of having his new breast feathers soaked again by his wife's torrent of tears!).

"But, I've got ..." she protested half-heartedly, only to be interrupted by her husband again.

"... and I've arranged it all,"he went on,"by sending a message by that nice friendly wood pigeon which lives in the poplar of Number 20; he seems like a decent sort. Offered to do the errand without any prompting from me. I just mentioned matters, and straight away he cooed his offer. We must ask him over for tea one day after we get back."

"But we can't just ..."she tried again.

"A few days in the country is what you need to buck you up," he continued, unable to be stopped. He knew that if he didn't give her the opportunity to throw in one or two excuses for not going, she would finally agree, and true enough, he kept talking for long enough eventually to make her give in and consent.

"When shall we ...?"she sighed finally.

"This afternoon is as good a time as any," his answer came quickly.

"This afternoon! But that's too ..." she blurted out, quite taken aback with the suddenness of it.

"Bags are packed, and everything's been seen to," he butted in again in assurance. You see, Mr T's reasoning was such that Mrs T, presented with nothing upon which to hang any doubts or problems, would have to give in, and by timing the visit for so soon, he would remove all chance for her to rethink and back out. So that was that!

Mrs T spent the rest of the morning in frenzied activity packing 'all those last minute things Mr T could possibly be expected to think of.'

Goodbyes said, with a little misgiving and apprehension on Mrs T's part at leaving the two boys to fend for themselves, the couple set off looking forward to their short break. She had no real reason to worry, her husband had assured her, as Furtive would be spending the whole time with Patience, and Fearless had many friends to visit and much to do. Lemuel, of course, would be keeping an eye on their home (if he remembered, that is), which would still be there when they returned.

The days following were quiet and beautiful indeed. Little activity was to be witnessed at Number 18 save the arrival of the new family to take over residence, and they moved in with the minimum amount of fuss and performance even though they arrived with two large removal vans.

The family drew up in an enormous black limousine with shiny chromium handles, bumper and hubcaps. So shiny were they that they seemed to be made of glass, reflecting the occasional flash of afternoon sun as it dashed from cloud to cloud. The lady of the family was exceedingly large, like an old-fashioned Spanish galleon in full sail, with great white billowing skirts and a huge mainsail of a hat trimmed with cream lace and flowers. She was, of course, admiral of the operation, directing her midshipman husband, who seemed to be in perpetual motion trying to keep track of their belongings as they skipped from van to house at an alarming rate.

There were two little boys as well (twins, to be precise) of about seven or eight. They wore high, brilliant white starched collars, held together with tie-pinned cravats of one of the more expensive public schools of the neighbourhood. They were so alike that their slightest movements were in unison; oiled black hair reflected the light; knife-edge pressed trousers creased at the same time in the same place. They were perfect (the sort of sickening perfection that makes you want to jump in a pool of mud next to them, or encourage a flock of seagulls to fly over them!).

Barrington and Ballantyne were their names; Algernon Barrington Carfax and Ballantyne Cecil Carfax, to be precise.

Underneath that sharp, newly-pressed and highly-polished exterior, however, there beat hearts of pure scheming naughtiness; not the naughtiness and mischief that most little boys get up to because that's what they are, but the naughtiness I'm sure you've all met. You know the type; break a window or scrump a pocketful of apples or chase next door's cat up a tree, and off they would scamper to hide behind mother's more than ample skirts from where they would put on that "I'm-a-good-little-boy" look. Consequently, they got away with everything.

They also had that uncanny sixth sense which kept them out of the way when mama was in one of her moods. Papa was the sort of chap most children would adore; kind, understanding and extremely fair.

Finally, by late afternoon, when the heat of the day was well past and that gentle coolness of early evening was beginning to caress the surrounding shrubs and trees, the removal (much to the intense relief of the removal men) was completed, and the galleon had had time for a cup of tea. She wandered round to the back of the domicile to survey the scene, husband in tow.

"That ... that ... thing," she boomed in a high-pitched warble, indicating the old oak, "will have to go. It takes up too much room, and it won't match up at all with the proper trees and flowers we shall grow. Arrange for it to be got rid of immediately, Henry."

"Yes dear. Right away dear," came the swift reply. Henry, as no doubt you will have guessed, was her hard-worked, badly-treated, downtrodden, irrepressible husband, and he was the real organiser and arranger of the family.

The next day, sharp and cracking in its clarity, brought out a sky so blue you would have been forgiven for thinking that the sun had changed colour, and that sky was the first to witness the early start of the felling of the oak tree!

Branch by branch, twig by twig, the wickedly sharp teeth of the screaming chain saw bit through the protesting wood as a child's teeth through marzipan. Relentlessly and mercilessly throughout the warm day, the once stately old oak was reduced to a pile of wood chippings and an even greater pile of logs. A profound silence, once the saw had done its worst, lay over the whole neighbourhood. The birds were quiet, stunned into silence by the activities of the day. Old Lemuel had been given a very rude and abrupt awakening from his early morning slumber after a long night's work excavating his beloved home.

He didn't really know what was happening, thinking as he did that some helpful relatives had sent an army of eager woodpeckers to give aid in his relentless quest for improved accommodation; until, that is, he emerged from one of his deeper chambers into his living room to find it was a beautiful day, with the sun streaming in!

"My word, what a beautiful ... day ... it ...!" he stammered to a halt, gazing at the ceiling that was no more. His living accommodation was now open to the sky where the saw had scythed its way through. That beautiful grained oak look to his ceiling had become a pastel shade of blue!

"But ..." he stuttered, attempting to scratch his head with his claw, parrot-fashion.

As he was trying to search for the words to express his surprise and annoyance at not having been consulted on any alterations or renovations, he started suddenly to move upwards with the whole of his abode about him, as if someone had turned on a lift to take him to the upper floors. Puzzlement would be something of an understatement to describe Lemuel's looks and feelings at that moment. It was a strange, funny and wonderful sight to see a huge chunk of oak tree, held by the great grappling teeth of a mechanical crane, with the relatively tiny head and beak of one very surprised woodpecker peering over the side vainly trying to assess the situation and to find the reason for his sudden going up in the world.

He spent the rest of the operation in the uppermost branches of the elm next door, sadly ruing the day such a catastrophe should happen to him of all people, a good, law-abiding neighbourly, friendly, (noisy), inoffensive woodpecker. He just didn't dare imagine what his dear friends the Twitcherlys would think, having asked him to keep an eye on things. Squatting squirrels were one thing, but chain saws and mechanical grabbers were entirely another. They would all have to apply for rehousing, or something, but he didn't quite know what or where.

The dust finally settled, and the tree gobblers removed their equipment and departed, leaving … a great, obvious, gaping gap in the air. The tree had been in that position, sapling and tree, for so long that, now that it had gone, if you looked hard and closely you could still see its ghostly outline. The contractors had made a mess of the garden where they had been with their heavy machinery and their large trampling feet, but that was something which could be easily repaired. The old oak could never be repaired or replaced. The removal of such an established resident would have serious consequences for many of the surrounding animals, birds and insects, and many of them mourned its passing. I suppose the old tree deposited many acorns about awaiting a proper time when they could germinate and grow (they had a habit of doing that, you know), but that would take years and years and years; time which was too long for the neighbourhood's residents.

Chapter Eleven

Days came and went as days often do, making a very sad period in an area where there had been only happiness. Apart from the untimely disappearance of the tree, the main unrest and disquiet was caused by those twin horrors, Barrington and Ballantyne Carfax.

They chased away all animals, set traps for squirrels, brought in cats to hide in the shrubbery to catch the birds, dug up hundreds of worms to use as bait, and generally caused a great deal of upset. In fact, so efficient were they, in the three days since the 'Removal of Tree Day', in harassing animal life, that by the end of that time none visited the garden of Number 18, leaving it strangely and uncannily quiet.

However, before they were driven out altogether, the animals had the last laugh.

The twins had chosen a fine warm day to unveil their masterpiece of harassment for the wildlife around. They had, in fact, slipped out under cover of darkness the night before to prepare their surprises. The strange thing about these two was that they never spoke to one another. They seemed to 'know' what each other was thinking or about to do. So everything they had planned was carried out in complete silence as they worked like two halves of a clockwork motor.

Behind the garage, next to the large potting shed, there was a huge water butt. Only, this morning, there wasn't. It had mysteriously disappeared.

The boys were out early, ready to enjoy their sport, catching the local wild stock unawares. Unfortunately for Barrington and Ballantyne the local 'wild stock' wasn't quite as stupid as they would have hoped. In fact, the animals had been expecting something big to happen, ever since they had first glimpsed the two, and so every night a watch-guard had been set at various points in the garden of Number 18. A couple of owls in the elm, the odd squirrel in the shrubbery, and others had closely observed the nocturnal antics of these two boys. With the arrival of the day all were ready, prepared, waiting expectantly.

After not so very long an ear-shattering screech, mingled with the sound of a body hitting water, was followed by its not-quite-as-loud echo nearby. The galleon appeared on the horizon, sailing at full speed to find out what had befallen her offspring, with her down-trodden husband close behind. The scene, when she had reached the place the old oak had occupied, stopped her in her rustling tracks, and with mouth agape, she was lost for words for the first time in her regal existence. Henry fought valiantly (with barely enough success) to suppress his mirth at the just 'accidents' that had caught up with his unruly and undeserving sons.

One of the little Bs (Ballantyne, I think) could be seen barely able to keep his streaming head above the surface of a small pond of water, and the other B (Barrington, of course) was performing spectacular gyrating exercises, upside-down, suspended by an ankle attached to a stout piece of rope hanging from the branch of the corner elm. Both were emitting alarming squeals for help which Mama could hardly ignore.

"Don't ... don't just stand there ... do ... something," she stammered almost purple with suppressed fright. If you've ever seen a great billowy lady purple with compressed emotion which was about to explode at any time, you would have done precisely what her long-suffering husband did - as he was told! (He was long-suffering, as you have seen). With the dexterity born of many years ducking his lady's anger, he removed one sorry, bedraggled and gasping heir from the water, and proceeded, quite unconcernedly, to disentangle its exact, dry replica from the branches above. Mama swept them from his grasp as soon as they were in sweeping distance, and hurried the 'poor dears' into the safety of her house to be revived, cosseted and generally restored to that sharp, shiny dignity which befitted their rank. Henry was left outside, door firmly locked against his audacious callousness, to clear up the mess, and generally to think about his situation.

You are, no doubt, wondering by now just a bit, how the 'little dears' came to find themselves in such a state – wet or hanging. Well, this is what happened...

They had decided to catch some of the livestock (beastly stuff it was, according to the two Bs), by various, cleverly hatched and well thought-out plots. The boys had managed to bury the water butt just to its rim in one of the holes left by the tree removers, and, filling it again to the rim using the hosepipe, they concealed its surface by delicate, finely balanced and positioned twigs and grasses. They had laid a lure of morsels of tasty food at its centre so as to catch some unsuspecting and unwary creature (the odd squirrel or two, or even perhaps some heavier bird) in the water.

The rope (stout string, actually) they had, again cleverly they had thought, fashioned in the way of a series of noose-like loops which would tighten over the birds' legs, head or any other part of other stupidly unsuspecting creatures, thereby making the Bs' fun complete. Unfortunately for Barrington and Ballantyne, the animals thereabouts had out-manoeuvred, out-foxed and out-witted them.

Ballantyne (or was it his brother?) had noticed with glee several animals (one squirrel and two blackbirds to be exact) rooting about near his tub. They came ever nearer to the juicy morsels on the top, much to his mounting excitement, but without actually having the goodness to venture on to the trap. His impatience overcame him somewhat, and he decided to hurry matters along a little. He performed what he considered to be a very clever out-flanking manoeuvre, by moving very quietly in behind the animals through the shrubbery (as quietly as a rhinoceros in a thicket!) to usher them into his trap.

As he approached to make his final thrust, several sparrows dive-bombed him from either side, taking him completely off guard. Not looking where he was going, he caught his toe in a protruding tree root and catapulted himself, head first, into the watery trap he had set for the poor, unsuspecting, but not so stupid animals!

At the same time, the other B, having climbed the elm to inspect his rope traps, was distracted by a thrush and a wren acting as if they had become lame - wing dragging and making distressed calls. His attention taken from his chosen path, he blundered into those so-well-concealed snares, to be caught, hanging about, by the ankles. The stupid, easily out-witted, easily-caught animals had triumphed yet again!

Rest assured, those particular little boys would not be playing tricks or pranks again - at least, not for a while.

Chapter the last

"Well, my dear," came Mr T's familiar voice as they rounded the far houses of Mulberry Road, "home again soon."

"Yes," his wife replied. "I've had a wonderfully restful time, but I shall be pleased to see my nest again. I hope our estimable Lemuel has kept a better eye ... on ... our ..." Her voice tailed off as she came in to land on the back guttering of the roof of Number 18, and looked over to where her home used to be. She looked across with wild disbelieving eyes at her husband who had a puzzled look on his face.

"But, where ...?" she went on.

"Hang on a bit," he replied. "We must have taken the wrong turning. I'll go and ..."

"No need; no need," a cracked voice sounded from just behind them on the tiles. It was Mr Micah, the Jackdaw. "It's been done; been done. The tree's gone, gone, gone. Far away. Nowhere to live; nowhere to go, eh? But we fixed 'em. Fixed 'em good, eh!" He stopped his chatter for a moment whilst he performed a jackdaw's version of a victory reel on the tiles, wings whirling, and claws clicking on the roof.

This was no comfort at all, however, for Mrs T, who finally burst into floods of tears, quite wetting her feathers through. Her husband tried valiantly to comfort her whilst suffering from shock himself. A new home could be found (he hoped), he tried to tell her. She didn't, of course, hear a word of it. She was too busy being upset.

Mr Twitcherly held his wife even more tightly, and closed his eyes fast shut. "I wish, oh I wish," he started, "that all this hadn't happened, and we had our home again."

He had hoped it was all a ghastly dream, and that when he opened his eyes, it would have all been put back to rights again.

He did open his eyes again after a few minutes, knowing that it wouldn't have changed, and it wasn't a nightmare. He would then have to set about finding a suitable new home. His wife's sobbing by this time had subsided; in fact, he couldn't hear it at all. As he opened his eyes he looked at his wife's face which wore an expression of utter amazement, staring as it was straight ahead of it. He turned and followed her gaze to be somewhat surprised himself in his turn.

The view that met his gaze was in fact quite astonishing. The garden before them was enormous, the boundaries of which the Ts could hardly see, they were so far away. Over to the back right hand corner (if that's what you could call it in a garden of this size), they could just make out what they thought to be a ... mountain stream? ... with rocks, pines and ... surely not! ... its own weather - cloud-capped mountains and all! But in miniature. But how...?

In the middle distance, but much further away than the back fence at Number 18, was a glorious elm in full leaf, sailing like a great green galleon, in the sky, with sails billowing in a stiff breeze. The lawns, of course, were not really lawns; more like green rolling countryside whose boundaries went on forever. Mr T would have considered they were in the country had they not tile and guttering under their claws.

"But ... I ... Uncle Eb ...?" Mr T stammered quite upset and perplexed by the whole affair, but stopped short when his wife interrupted him.

"Look!" she exclaimed, "over there in that elm. There's someone waving, I think. Do you think it's us they want?" And for the first time in her life she took a momentous decision.

"Come on!" she burst out, surprising herself as well as her husband with her impetuosity. "Let's go!" and with that she launched herself from the roof, leaving a very surprised male bird behind her. He did, of course, follow, eventually, when he had overcome the shock, and caught up with her about half-way to the elm.

"Look!" he pointed out as he drew level with her; "on that bough above left. It's ... and ..."

"Yes! Yes!" she chirped with joy and glee, almost forgetting to flap her wings, but she managed to remember before she lost too much height. "My boys! My boys!"

Their landing was perfect, right on target beside four other sparrows on a broad landing area in front of a winding stairway leading to a highly polished oak door. There was a brass knob off to one side and a small semi-circular window at the top with darkened glass.

You will no doubt have realised by now that this was the elm of Old...

" ... Benjamin," Furtive introduced the old bird, "and this is Patience, his daughter, and ... my wife." Fearless also was there, a big grin on his beak.

"Oh, my dear," Mrs T said, putting a wing around Patience, and bursting into tears (of joy this time) again.

"But ... you're ..."Mr Twitcherly began, puzzled.

"... like Ebeneezer?" Benjamin finished his question with a slight smile behind his half-moon spectacles.

"Yes ... How ...?"Mr T went on again.

"But haven't you guessed already?"the old bird went on."I am Ebeneezer, if you like, and he is me."

Then with a swish of his tassel, a twitch of his beak feathers, and a flash of his spectacles, he whisked the whole assembly into his house.

That, then, could easily have been that. But not quite...

The surprising thing was that everything had been planned and worked out whilst the Twitcherlys were away. Old Lemuel had been pressed to excavate the most sumptuous nest hole ever (apart from Benjamin's, of course) for Mr and Mrs T to move to. Furtive and Patience had their own also, and Lemuel had been given leave to complete the gathering by choosing his own site - all in the Great Elm of Benjamin. There could have been no happier family gathering anywhere.

Old Benjamin, you know, was a magical bird. Everything under his wing was protected and looked after, and, if I'm not very much mistaken, I think that they're all there still, in that same elm ... somewhere.

So, if ever you're in one of those enormous gardens with old trees and so on, look a little more closely at that great elm and, you never know, you might see ...

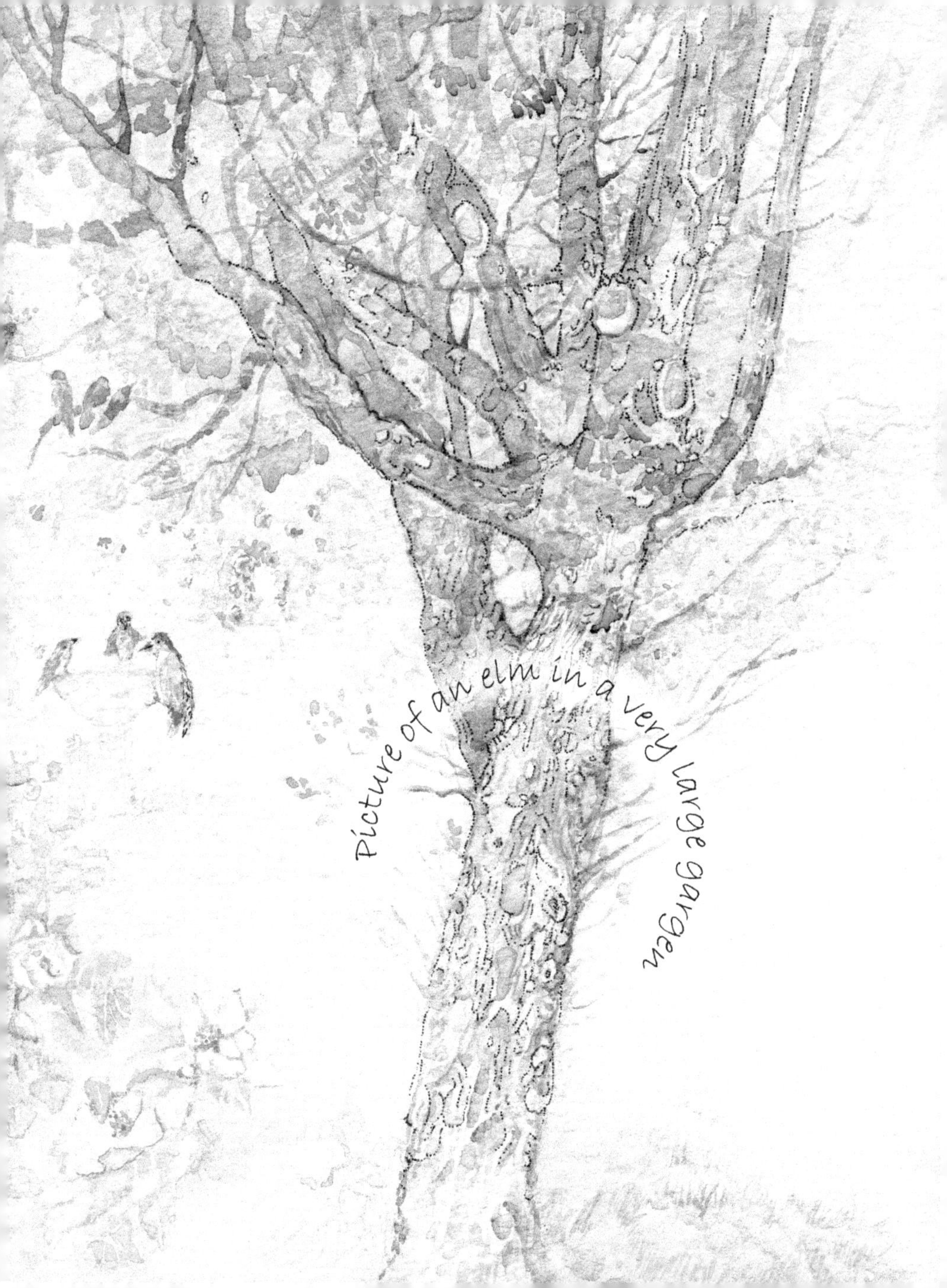
Picture of an elm in a very Large gargen

THE END

About the Author

Frank English

Born in 1946 in the West Riding of Yorkshire's coalfields around Wakefield, he attended grammar school where he enjoyed sport rather more than academic work. After three years at teacher training college in Leeds, Frank became a teacher in 1967. He spent a lot of time during his teaching career entertaining children of all ages, a large part of which was through telling stories, and encouraging them to escape into a world of imagination and wonder. He found some of his most troubled youngsters to be very talented poets. Frank has always had a wicked sense of humour, which has blossomed during the time he has spent with his present wife. This sense of humour also allowed many youngsters to survive often difficult and upsetting home environments.

Recently, Frank retired after forty years working in schools with young people, most of whom had significantly disrupted lives due to behavioural disorders and poor social environments, generally brought about through circumstances beyond their control. At the same time as moving from leafy lane suburban middle class school teaching to residential schooling for the emotionally and behaviourally disturbed in the early 1990s, a change in circumstance provided the spur to achieve ambitions. Supported by his wife, Denise, he achieved a Master's degree in his mid-forties and a PhD at the age of fifty-six; something he had always wanted to do.

Now enjoying glorious retirement, Frank spends as much time as life will allow writing, reading and travelling.